CLASH IN THE BALTIC

CLASH IN THE BALTIC

Duncan Harding

Severn House Large Print
London & New York

This first large print edition published in Great Britain 2005 by
SEVERN HOUSE LARGE PRINT BOOKS LTD of
9-15 High Street, Sutton, Surrey, SM1 1DF.
First world regular print edition published 2004 by
Severn House Publishers, London and New York.
This first large print edition published in the USA 2006 by
SEVERN HOUSE PUBLISHERS INC., of
595 Madison Avenue, New York, NY 10022.

ESSEX COUNTY LIBRARIES

British Library Cataloguing in Publication Data

Harding,   Duncan,   1926 -
    Clash in the Baltic. - Large print ed.
    1.   World War, 1939 – 1945 - Commando operations -
         Great Britain - Fiction
    2.   World War, 1939 – 1945 - Prisoners and prisons, German - Fiction
    3.   War stories
    4.   Large type books
    I.   Title
    823.9'14 [F]

    ISBN-10:   0-7278-7478-0

Printed and bound in Great Britain by
MPG Books Ltd, Bodmin, Cornwall.

In wartime, truth is so precious that she should always be attended by a bodyguard of lies.

Winston Churchill

Author's Note

'Let's face it, Duncan,' the publisher had said, breathing red wine fumes all over me, 'this one is a real winner. After all, it'll have Ian Fleming in it, remember.' We were coming to the end of a long, watery lunch and now he smiled winningly. He always does when he tries to land me with another of his 'best-selling epics', as he calls them.

'So?' I'd asked, playing it cool. I was trying to show him I couldn't be bought that easily, especially on the advances he pays to his authors. You know, gentle reader, sometimes I think he bloody well expects me to pay *him* for the privilege of writing his bloody 'epics'!

'But, Duncan,' he'd pleaded, pulling a face as if he couldn't understand the world any more, 'Ian Fleming. *The* Ian Fleming, who wrote all those James Bond books. I don't have to tell you that the movies of Mr Fleming's books [I noted that *Mr* Fleming and told myself that things were getting serious] have made more money than any others in the whole history of Hollywood.' He signalled the creaking old waiter for more *rouge* and I swear at that moment his fingers began to twitch, as if he were already counting the dosh he'd make if he managed to talk me into writing the latest 'epic'. 'Think of it seriously, very seriously,' he'd continued. 'You know I'm right, Duncan.' (When my publisher starts with his 'Duncan' or, even worse, the old 'my dear Duncan', you know you've got to start watching him like a hawk. He's out for the kill.) 'You've got the creator of the world-famous James Bond movies in a true-life adventure story set in World War Two. I mean, Duncan, what more can a writer ask for, I beg you.' Here he'd thrown up his hands in despair as if he couldn't understand the world any more.

I sniffed. Yes, I did. I must admit I'm very good at sniffing, especially when I've had plenty of free booze and have got the publisher virtually down on his knees pleading with me. Soon, if I played my cards right, I thought, he might even offer me more money. Things like that have been known to happen, or so I've been told by other old-time hacks.

'You mean,' I'd said, 'I should do something on that old Etonian toff who wrote fairy tales for adults?' And then I'd really turned the knife in the wound, yes – although I am normally the milk of human kindness, as you know, gentle reader – I really did. I added, 'Besides, there aren't any adventure stories set in World War Two, only nasty rotten accounts of bloody mayhem. That's not adventure.'

But by that time my publisher (helped along by the red plonk) wasn't listening. So in the end I bought the idea. Another 'epic' had been born. Naturally I couldn't stomach Ian Fleming, James Bond and all that guff and I had had my few minutes of playing hard to get. But as always with us hacks I was broke and I needed money. I mean, this new woman of mine goes through it like a bloody fur-coated whippet. She's in and out of Marks and Sparks as if she's a majority shareholder in the blooming place. So there it was: Ian Fleming and enough money for a month's supply of G & Ts and another dose of 'Look, darling, what I just picked up at M & S for *two* for the price of one!' That woman will believe anything.

Mind you, I must admit that when I'd cleared away all the bull about Ian Fleming, it *was* a good, if very nasty story. You see, Fleming had been a wartime commander with British Naval Intelligence. He was really a chairborne warrior – you know, one of those blokes who sit behind a desk and send other blokes to their death. Supposedly he'd been behind bringing the Führer's deputy, Hess, to Britain and had held regular conferences with old 'Father Christmas' (Admiral Canaris, head of the German Secret Service, to you, gentle reader). And there was that bloody fantastic tale of how Fleming had brought Martin Bormann, Hitler's 'Brown Eminence', to Britain after the war when he had been lying long dead under the ruins of Berlin. That was all tosh, which Fleming encouraged. Chairborne warriors are like that.

The reality of his one overseas operation was in fact totally different from those daring tales in the Sapper tradition. In early '45, Churchill had ordered that a handful of brave SOE* women operatives under sentence of death in Nazi Germany were to be brought out. The operation was to be carried out under the command of the SOE's rival service, the Secret Intelligence Service, and Ian Fleming at Naval Intelligence.

Special Operations Executive, an Intelligence organization, created by Churchill in 1940.

The operation had gone drastically wrong. *On purpose!* 'C', the head of the Secret Intelligence Service – who would later feature as 'M' in many of Fleming's post-war novels – had, with Fleming's aid, effectively torpedoed the rescue attempt. It is hardly believable that our own people would do anything like that: one intelligence organization sacrificing the agents of another intelligence organization to the enemy. But as you know, gentle reader, the events of our own time have shown to what lengths such organizations will go to save the necks of their own bosses and their political masters. Poor Britain!

Anyway, this is their tale. It's not pleasant, but then, as I always say, there weren't any pleasant tales in those days, were there?

Duncan Harding, Schleswig-Holstein,
Germany, 2004

Prelude to Murder

They were shooting the prisoners again. They always did after dawn.

The guards, all middle-aged, comfortable men, fat and jolly in the crude SS way, who could have been anyone's favourite grandfather, felt themselves too old to get up and shoot the ragged, starving prisoners in the pre-dawn cold. They waited till they'd warmed up with a canteen of steaming hot ersatz coffee laced with a strong schnapps. Then they got down to the boring routine business of 'liquidating' yet another batch of their wretched prisoners.

Back when the women had arrived from the camps in France, which had been evacuated before the advancing Anglo-Americans, the SS guards had not been allowed to use such liberal amounts of ammunition, and shootings were infrequent. Only visiting officers had been allowed to whip out their pistols and kill at random a few of the wretches in their ragged pyjama-like

13

uniforms. For Lofty it had been like some of the grandees at her father's estate before the war, who ignored the rules of the 'shoot' and banged away at anything in sight.

Then back in February, when they had finally arrived at this camp on the East Prussian coast, the guards had lined the prisoners up in batches of twenty against a wall. Above them, at about two metres, there were hooks from which a short slip-noose dangled. With their hands tied behind their backs there was little the condemned men could do when the guards had placed the nooses around their necks and pulled. For the watching women, the men's deaths seemed to take a hell of a time. The prisoners wet themselves and did frantic jigs with their legs until finally their heads slumped to one side and their tongues hung out like pieces of purple leather. Thereafter they were raised by the elevator and taken to the ovens for disposal and there was peace till the next dawn.

Sometimes this terrible strangulation procedure took too long for the middle-aged guards, especially in February when the wind seemed to be blowing straight from Siberia and the corpses hanging from the nooses would freeze stiff as boards within minutes. Then they would beat the prisoners to death, bashing out their brains with what reminded Lofty of the potato-masher that their cook, Ma Titmus, had used in the estate kitchens back before the war.

Fat Otto, the *Oberscharführer* in charge of their SS guards, didn't like the beatings. As he complained more than once to Lisa, who spoke fluent German (fortunately the German authorities didn't know she had been born a Jew, not fifty miles away from where they were now), 'It's too hard work for us at our age, Fraulein Lisa:' Then he'd rub his fat shoulder. 'My poor arm aches something terrible. The big shots over there in admin just don't know how it takes it out of folk at my time of life.' And he would look at her, expecting some sort of sympathy from her. She would nod and, with a sheer effort of will, fight back the burning tempta-tion to slap him across his rosy, well-nourished pig's face.

This morning, with the Russian guns thundering even louder to the east and the stench of ordure burning – everyone in the great sprawling camp seemed to suffer from dysentery and what the guards called 'thin shits' – worse than ever, they shot a double batch of the emaciated skeletons who had once been men and women, perhaps even children, and now they were using machine guns instead of rifles. As Lofty told her best friend, Rosie Macpherson, the Scottish radio operator – whom the guards called *Titten* due to her enormous bosom, which she had managed to preserve despite the starvation rations – 'They want to get rid of us quick, Rosie. We're an embarrassment to them. We've got to disappear.'

'Aye, I ken, Lofty,' Rosie replied stoutly. 'But they're nae gonna get rid of Mrs Macpherson's handsome daughter that quick.'

Lofty grinned. 'That's the way to talk, Rosie. Don't let them get you down.'

'Them buggers'll never get *me* down,' Rosie replied as the chatter of the machine guns ceased. Now the base of the wall was filled with the dead and the dying, and here and there one of the men, fighting for life till the last, tried to drag himself away, dribbling blood-red excrement behind his sagging, wasted body.

'Goon in the block.' Nellie (Dean) warned as the stamp of Fat Otto's boots came echoing down the stone corridor. 'Watch yourselves, girls. Here comes God's gift to womanhood.'

The six women gave a weary laugh. As fast as they could in their emaciated state, they smoothed their hair and pulled their striped skirts down. Rosie, the best nourished of them all, puffed up her chest. 'Tits all right, ladies?' she queried.

They laughed again and Lofty, the product of Cheltenham Ladies' College, who six years before had been a social beauty – presented at Court, surrounded by handsome, rich young men, most of whom were now dead in battle – told herself what good chaps they all were. Ever since they had been captured one by one during 1943 and '44 in France, they had stuck together. They had suffered beatings, torture, week-long interrogations, French jails and German concentration camps, knowing that any dawn could be their last. If they had been downhearted, they had never shown it. Instead they had fought back, telling themselves that it was the only way to keep their spirits up, and perhaps even save their lives – they were all under sentence of death for espionage. They knew the Germans respected courage and the kind of cheerful cheekiness and irreverance that Lofty thought was uniquely British.

Oberscharführer Breitner jingled his keys in warning. As he said in his fractured English, of which the Savoy's ex-pastry cook was so proud, 'I am not wanting you ladies with your knickers down or something.' Next

17

moment he opened the door of their cell and raised his pudgy hand to his cap and saluted, stating, 'I hope you have sleeped well, my ladies.' It was part of the ritual. No one ever slept more than a couple of hours in that dreadful place, where men died at all hours of the night.

Lisa played their little game too. She clicked to attention as best she could with her swollen legs and cried, as if she were a member of the SS herself. *'Melde gehorsamt, Oberscharführer, sechs Gefangenen – und ein Pisseimer, leer.'* She indicated the empty latrine bucket in the corner, which as a matter of honour they never used at night; it was all part and parcel of their defiance.

'Ladies, ladies.' Fat Otto spread his fat pastry cook's hands. 'I beg you ... Please.' He reached in the pocket of his ill-fitting grey tunic with the tarnished runes of the SS at the collar. 'Cigarettes ... Russian cigarettes, I have for you.' Politely he handed the packet round and equally politely they accepted one each and bowed or curtseyed their thanks. When Fat Otto had first taken charge of them, they had debated whether they should accept his cheap looted cigarettes or not. In the end they had decided to do so. Six cigarettes could buy them six slices of black bread from the communist

18

'kitchen bulls', who were part of the communist underground of the German prisoners. A slice of bread per woman might mean they'd live to see another of these dreadful dawns.

For a few moments they admired their cigarettes while Fat Otto watched them, pleased that he seemed to have made these high-born English ladies happy as he had once done in the Savoy with his special *Bienenstich*, *Kaiserschmarren* and the like★. Admittedly every now and again his red, piggy eyes flashed to Rosie's huge breasts, which he would have dearly loved to fondle. But although he had power of life and death over these English spies, he knew he couldn't. He'd save his sexual energies for the whores from all over Europe with which the SS brothel was filled. Indeed now, as the war seemed to be going ever more badly for the Reich, and he guessed he'd soon be returned home to the domestic charms of his Mutti, who knitted her own cosy woollen knickers, he was gathering enough sexual experiences and memories for the lean, boring years to come, taking a different whore from a different country every night – when he was capable.

★German and Austrian pastries.

Lofty, who was the unofficial leader of these condemned women, guessed it was the opportune time to ask her usual question, while Fat Otto was still in a good mood. For even the fat ex-pastry cook was subject to the same kind of irrational moods that seemed to afflict all the guards. One moment they could be tickling some child under the chin like an affectionate father with his favourite offspring; the next they'd draw a pistol and shoot the child dead for no apparent reason.

'How is the war going, *Oberscharführer?* Have the Ivans broken!' She meant the advancing Russians fighting to reach the Baltic coast.

Fat Otto suddenly looked grim. 'I must disappoint you, gracious miss. I know you want a German victory over the Russki beast. It is not to be.' He looked to left and right swiftly, afraid he might be overheard – then even the SS were frightened of the all-powerful Gestapo. Satisfied he wasn't, he lowered his voice and said, 'It is rumoured, gracious miss, that soon we must leave. The Russkis are coming close – very close.'

The tall spy caught her breath. 'By land?' she asked quickly. She knew that most of the German civilians trekking westwards before the advancing Russians never made it. If the worst winter in twenty-five years didn't finish them off, marauding Russian Cossacks, Allied fighter-bombers and myriad other dangers would. In their particular situation, weakened as they were by weeks behind bars, starvation rations and with no warm clothing save for their prison garb, they didn't stand a chance in hell. They'd never make it more than a day or two before they'd collapse in the snow, leaving their bones to lie in some godforsaken Pomeranian meadow with not even a crude wooden cross to mark their passing.

Fat Otto looked embarrassed. He flushed a deeper red and for an instant he lowered his gaze like some naughty schoolboy with a bad conscience. 'No,' he stuttered. 'Not by land.'

'By sea?' Lofty asked eagerly. She knew that the German Navy was evacuating key soldiers and civilians from these East Prussian ports on the Baltic and the area of Schleswig-Holstein, which was still in German hands.

Fat Otto didn't answer immediately. She could see from the look on his face that his mind was on some inner conflict; simple soul that he was, he couldn't hide his emotions and mental problems. After what seemed a long time, as outside the work

21

groups began to form, the communist German *Kapos*, who did the dirty work for the SS, cracking their whips and wielding their clubs, crying, *'Los, ihr Schweine ... an die Arbeit'*, Fat Otto said, 'Well yes, gracious miss, I suppose ... by sea ... In special transports.'

Her heart sank at the mention of 'special'. Everything bad that had happened to her since she had been abandoned by the French Maquis in the Orleans area and captured by a *Spezialkommando*, the previous September somehow seemed to have been associated with the word 'special'. Hastily she asked, *'Oberscharführer*, what kind of special transports?'

Obviously the ex-pastry cook felt he had said enough. He tugged his hat straight. 'I speak no more,' he snapped, very much the SS NCO now. 'I have duty. You know as we Germans say, "Dienst ist Dienst, Schnaps ist Schnaps." '* With that he saluted and was gone, almost forgetting to lock the cell door behind him in his haste.

After he had gone, the women fell silent, listening to the shuffle of the barefoot prisoners through the snow and slush, heading to their work from which a goodly

* 'Duty is duty, schnapps is schnapps'.

number wouldn't return after their twelve-hour shift on starvation rations was finally over. Each of the women was preoccupied with her own thoughts and problems – and they weren't pleasant. Then, just before the female Kapo came to blow her whistle and command sharply: 'All right, English ladies, outside to latrines for pissing,' Lofty said, her voice urgent, 'Girls, they're going to murder us … We're destined to be drowned at sea…'

ONE

The Fleming Commando

One

'Your tea, sir,' the pretty teenage Wren said, the cups rattling on the Ministry of Works tray. 'I'll attend to the fire, sir.' She indicated the miserable few pieces of coal flickering in the black grate.

Commander Ian Fleming would have preferred a double Scotch – it was so cold in Room 39, the Naval Intelligence HQ in Whitehall – but she was a pretty innocent little thing, just ready to lose her innocence, so he turned on all his considerable charm and said, 'How very good of you. Yes, please attend to the fire. It's freezing in here.'

She flushed and turned, while Fleming told himself that his boss, the admiral in charge of the Royal Navy's Intelligence Service, hadn't lost his talent for picking girls to work in HQ who, as he put it, 'are well-bred, Ian, and have pretty damn good legs'.

This one definitely had very good legs and a pert little bum to go with them. As she bent down to kindle the dying fire, he

27

caught a glimpse of white flesh above the non-regulation sheer silk stockings. More, her delightful buttocks were clearly outlined against the tight navy-blue skirt. He swallowed and licked lips that were suddenly dry. Only two weeks ago, when he had visited his 30th Commando in northern Germany where they were currently stalled, awaiting orders for the final attack to the Baltic, he had personally seduced a German Wren and then had punished her with his little whip, which he carried with him at all times, just in case. For a moment he let his imagination wander, trying to visualize those pert buttocks naked, the girl bent over the back of a chair as he brought the lash down across her bare white flesh.

Then as he heard the stamp of heavy shoes coming round the corner, indicating that the admiral was on his way – he always walked as if he were still pacing the quarterdeck of the battleship he had once commanded – Fleming reluctantly dismissed that delightful image. In due course, if he were allowed to stay in the capital long enough, he'd work hard to make it all come true; he hadn't had a virgin for quite some time now.

The admiral was his usual red-faced bluff self. He swung round the door, spotted the girl kneeling at the fire, barked, 'Off you go, girl. Have to discuss something most secret with the commander here', shook Fleming's hand with a grip that hurt and added, 'Got one of your posh gaspers for me, Ian? ... Dying for a spit-and-a-draw. The frocks are driving me barmy.'

Fleming gave his lopsided smile, produced his silver cigarette case and offered one of his gold-rimmed cigarettes that he had had made for him specially in Bond Street. 'I'll swear, sir, you only like to see me on account of these hand-rolled cigs.'

The admiral ignored the comment. He accepted Ian Fleming's light and barked, 'Well, what's with the Hun special sub? Churchill's awfully keen to get the details before the Russkis get their filthy paws on it. Your Thirty Commando chaps – are they any closer to snatching it?'

For a moment the younger man didn't answer. He took his time fitting the expensive hand-rolled cigarette into the ivory-handled cigarette holder he affected. He knew the admiral had been instrumental in allowing him to set up his special commando, which kept up with the leading troops of the British Liberation Army in north-west Europe. Its job was to seek out German naval and other military secrets before the

Russians advancing from the east into Germany did; even before their erstwhile allies the Americans did. The Yanks had teams everywhere, scouring their areas of operations looking for secrets and, more particularly, for the Germans, Nazi or otherwise, who were in charge of those secrets. As the admiral had commented cynically more than once: 'As long as it's new and free, even if it were made by Hitler himself, they'd be after it – *and him*. Then off to the Land of the Free.'

But the admiral was at the beck and call of the politicos – the 'frocks', he called them – and seemingly they were currently breathing down his neck to discover the whereabouts of the new radical German Walther submarine. But at this moment that sub was on the other side of the River Elbe and Fleming knew, hardcore Nazi and patriot that Walther was, he'd take the sub out to sea and sink her in the Baltic as soon as any danger of its capture loomed.

Now he explained the position to the admiral, who listened attentively – for him – and without interruption until Fleming was finished. 'So we're a bit between the devil and the deep blue sea, Ian,' he commented thoughtfully. 'The Hun will keep on working on the sub as long as we don't start to

30

advance. When we do, the Hun will destroy it if it's not ready to be handed over to the Japs. That's Winnie's worry. If the Japs get their hands on the Walther sub and start copying it in large numbers, our attack on the little yellow men as soon as the war in Europe is over is going to be tricky, decidedly so.' He rubbed his massive square jaw pensively.

Outside they were putting up the barrage balloons once more. London was still under attack from the German V-2 rockets and the barrage balloons, which gave absolutely no protection against the enemy's deadly new weapon, were launched routinely to make the Londoners believe that everything was being done for their protection. In fact there was no defence against these monstrous missiles falling out of space without warning.

Fleming must have shown his contempt on his lean, cynical face, for the admiral said, 'I know, I know, Ian. But we've got to do something, *anything* just as we of Naval Intelligence and your Thirty Commando have to do with that bloody Hun sub. It's for that reason I'm going to loan your Commando our latest secret weapon – the Skimmer.'

'*Skimmer?*' Fleming echoed, puzzled.

'Never heard of it. What is it, sir?'

'Well, they've been working on the skimmer project since 1944 down at Pompey. I think we've pinched the idea from the Eyeties – they're working on it with us now as – er co-belligerents. And we've added a few wrinkles of our own...'

Fleming let him talk. The admiral was an admirable fellow and usually very brisk in the best quarterdeck manner, but when he got on to some hobby horse, Fleming knew, he would ride the bloody thing to death. Thus it was due to his chief's talkativeness that Fleming wasn't to learn just yet what the skimmer was or how the mysterious new craft was to be employed.

For just as Fleming had decided that he was losing patience and was about to ask what the bloody thing really was there was a great whooshing sound. An instant later it was followed by a noise so tremendous and frightening that it seemed all the waters and winds in the world had combined in a mighty conflict, ready to wipe out for good this abomination to God, this war-torn world.

Fleming felt himself choking. The very air seemed to be being dragged out of his lungs. He wavered. He could stand no more. He tumbled to the floor as the door flew open to reveal the nubile little Wren sprawled dead, her plump thighs spread in one last sexual invitation. Fleming caught a last glimpse of her as a dark veil descended upon his gaze, his final thought being, 'I must keep on breathing ... I must ... breathe...' Then he lapsed into unconsciousness.

It may have been an hour, perhaps even more, but hurt as he was Fleming had no time to find out later. Slowly, very slowly, he started to realize that he was still alive. Dark shadows were all round, scrambling over brick rubble and debris: friendly shadows, who called out, offering succour, help, mentioning names he didn't know. His own voice seemed very far away too, as he said weakly, 'I'm over here ... please ... please help...'

Five minutes later the admiral, his forehead caked with dried blood, and others were pulling him free, while a fussy little naval doctor was pressing him all over to check whether any bones were broken, though Fleming thought the little Jewish medic's motives might be construed somewhat differently. Thereafter someone was feeding him a stiff drink and he was trying to keep his gaze from the dead Wren, her body covered with a blanket, but those black-clad legs still visible, and the admiral was explaining that a nearby building had been hit by a salvo of V-2, fired from 'somewhere in Holland'.

But by then, Fleming was sufficiently recovered from his ordeal to snarl, 'I don't give a fuck, old chap, whether or not they were fired from Outer Manchuria. All I want is that someone attempts to deal with their launching pads toot sweet.'

It was then that the admiral said, 'Maybe you've been picked to do the same, Ian?'

'What do you mean, sir?'

By way of an answer, the admiral held up a piece of paper so that he could read it in the dusty gloom of the bomb-damaged building and said, 'Urgent signal, for you *personal*, Ian.' He made the 'personal' sound very important. Fleming wondered why. A moment or two later he found out.

The admiral went on with 'Report to Chequers most immediately this day—'

'Chequers!' Fleming stuttered.

The admiral beat him to it. 'It's signed – by *Churchill*,' he said, his normally bluff manner barely concealing his own surprise. He lowered the signal and added, Now why in the name of Christ, Ian, would the prime minister want to see you, eh?'

But even Fleming, a man soon to be

celebrated for his vivid imagination in those novels that would go round the world and be made in movies long after their author had been forgotten, had no answer for that overwhelming question. All he could manage to say was, 'I suppose if I'm going to see the PM, I'd better try to rustle up a clean uniform, sir.'

The admiral nodded, apparently too surprised himself to make any further comment.

Five minutes later Fleming, still shaken, was limping down the debris-littered grand stairs to the waiting Humber staff car, while outside they were laying out the bodies of the dead to be taken away to the mortuary. For a moment Fleming let his eyes rest on the body of the dead Wren. This time he noticed she had a bad ladder in her right stocking. Idly he wondered what they'd cost on the black market. Moments later he was seated in the back of the big Humber with a plaid blanket draped around his legs by an attentive chauffeur. And by then he'd forgotten the Wren and the ladder in her stocking.

Two

It was Fat Otto who had made the women decide they had to do something before it was too late. He had staggered into the women agents' special *Barracke* early one evening as they huddled together in their tight bunks, covered with sacking and rags, trying to keep warm. Naturally he had made his usual jokes about women in prison turning to each other for sexual solace. They had ignored them. As far as most of them were concerned, they hadn't had a sexual thought for months. How could they with their dangerous job? Not to mention the starvation rations that their captors had given them.

Fat Otto had obviously been over to the SS brothel. He smelled of raw sex and drink. As was customary with the women agents, trained to assess people all the time – their lives might depend upon it – they had noticed Fat Otto had begun to drink more heavily of late. Sometimes he was even

36

drunk on duty, a serious offence in the SS. It could only mean, they had concluded, that the pudgy ex-Savoy pastry cook was worried. That evening, talking more than usual due to the schnapps he had drunk at the SS brothel, it became clear that Fat Otto definitely was worried.

'Ladies,' he said, slurring his words, 'I think we are move. I have just talked in a place...' He lowered his gaze as if he were suddenly ashamed. 'A naughty place, with sailors from Sweden.'

Lofty had flashed a warning glance at *Titten*. She knew the outspoken Scot. She mouthed the word 'Swedish', as if it were important, which it was. Sweden was a neutral country just on the other side of the Baltic. Up until recently most Swedes had been pro-German and Lofty had guessed Englishwomen like themselves could expect little help from that quarter. Now with Germany obviously losing the war, the Swedish attitude had clearly changed. Perhaps, she had reasoned that March evening, these Swedish sailors using the SS brothel might be of some use to them. She had given the drunken Fat Otto her toothy upper-class smile and said, 'Please, *Oberscharführer*, speak more. The Swedish sailors?'

'*Ja*,' Fat Otto had responded. 'They come

to help us. We must all go. Every ship is ... er ... mustered. Is that correct?'

'Yes, *Oberscharführer*,' Lofty had agreed hastily. 'Even Swedish ships.'

He had nodded, his fat jowls wobbling and what looked like tears welling up in his pale-blue eyes. 'And then we must go the Front.'

'You? The other guards?' the women had asked in unison.

Lofty asked with sudden sharpness, 'And what is to happen to us? Who will guard us, *Oberscharführer*?'

But Fat Otto had not been prepared to answer that question, even when Rosie had thrust out those still magnificent breasts of hers to impress him and keep him there in the freezing, bug-ridden *barracke*. Instead he had wobbled away into the night, still bewailing his fate and the dreadful possibility that soon he must go to the Front – certain death for any member of Himmler's elite SS.

That night – the silence broken only by the chatter of the machine guns as some poor wretch committed suicide by leaving his hut and approaching the wire where the guards in their towers, bored by the long night watch, were only too eager to break the monotony by slaughtering the prisoners – the women discussed the appearance of

38

the Swedes in the camp and the fact that Fat Otto and his middle-aged subordinates would soon be relieved of the 'burden' of guarding them.

'Although I'm only guessing,' Lofty had stated, 'if Fat Otto's lot won't be guarding us much longer, and Hitler's sending even them to the Front, then who *is* going to guard us?'

In the flickering light of their stub of precious candle, she had let her question sink in, gazing at their pale, emaciated faces in the flickering yellow light, each woman huddled close to the next, perhaps on account of the cold, but also perhaps with sudden fear.

In the end she answered her own question. Softly she said, 'Perhaps we won't need to be guarded when they relieve Fat Otto, girls.'

They were all realists. They had gone into the business knowing the risks. Back in the autumn of 1944, when they had been captured, most of them hadn't expected to survive very long. They had told themselves that one day soon it would be the dawn reveille, a hasty cigarette, perhaps a priest's blessing if they were lucky and then the slow march to the bullet-pocked wall, the blindfold, the harsh order of the officer commanding the firing squad – and then oblivion. But when that had not happened, they experienced renewed hope. They were going be saved after all. Now Fat Otto's words had reminded them just how vulnerable they still were.

'You mean,' Lisa began and then she had realized from the looks on their faces what they had been thinking and she had stopped abruptly. In the end it had been Rosie who, in that outspoken, tough Scottish manner of hers, had brought the matter out into the open. She had snapped, almost as if she were angry with her fellow prisoners, 'Ach awa with ye! Enough patter. If they're gonna kill us, what can we do to stop yon bastards?'

Her words awakened them to the gravity of the situation, but it was not until the next night, with the Russian guns rumbling in the distance, the horizon to the east, where the Front was, occasionally lightening up with the pink spurts of explosions, that they made their decision.

As usual it had been Lofty who articulated it. 'If you agree, we approach the Swedes ... those Swedish seamen that Fat Otto talked about. If the Hun can bribe them to work for them in the Baltic, then we should be able to bribe them with what we've got – you know, girls.' She'd blushed a little at that and, as hardened as they all were through the years of the war and their long months of imprisonment, most of them had lowered their gaze, too. 'We'll see what Radel can do for us, eh, girls?'

Kapo Radel had come the next night. The *Kapo* wore the same dirty striped pyjamas that they did, and at the beginning of his imprisonment – when most of the German Communist Party members had been arrested by Germany's new Nazi masters – he had suffered the same sort of beatings that all of the inmates had. Most of his teeth had been knocked out then so that he slurred his words badly and he was difficult to understand. There was only one thing that distinguished Radel from the others in the camp; he was well nourished and beefy. Underneath the thin material of his pyjamas his muscles rippled visibly. When he slapped the bull's pizzle that he carried in place of the usual whip it cracked loudly; there was plenty of strength behind the movement. 'Well?' he demanded from Lisa, who was to act as their spokeswoman. 'What do you want, woman?' He wiped the back of his dirty hand across his mouth as if to hide the gaps in his teeth, suddenly conscious he was a man surrounded by a number of young women, and one or two of them pretty at that.

Lisa took the plunge. In German she said, 'We want to meet some men, *Herr Kapo*.'

He looked at her as if she were crazy. '*Men?* What do you want men for?'

Lisa, the well-brought-up daughter of a professor of natural philosophy at the University of Cologne, didn't hesitate. She made an obscene gesture, poking her dirty forefinger through a hole formed by the thumb and forefinger of her other hand. 'For that. If we're going to die, we want to do that for perhaps one last time.'

For a moment Radel was too astonished to speak. Finally he gasped. '*I'm* a man. You've got me.' He grabbed the front of his dirty pyjamas.

She shook her shaven head. 'No. I'll be polite, *Herr Kapo*. You're one of us. You haven't got the strength.' She indicated the bull's pizzle dangling fat, heavy, but soft from his right hand, as if that signified everything. 'We want young men with meat on them, plenty of vigour. You know you were young once yourself.'

Behind her, as if to indicate what they wanted, Rosie thrust out those mighty breasts of hers, the nipples sticking through the thin material of her prison uniform. 'Some man who doesn't stink of this place,' she said in English.

Kapo Radel might not understand the language, but he understood the gesture. His eyes narrowed. 'Where am I to find men for you?' he asked. 'Why should I, even if I could? What's in it for me?'

Lofty could have shouted with glee. They'd got him! They'd heard through the camp's grapevine that Radel was a greedy man; that he could be bribed, as long as it didn't come to the attention of his fellow communists, who ran the place under the command of the SS. 'Lisa, tell him,' she said hastily, 'that we could make him rich, if he would help us.' Swiftly the Jewish girl translated her leader's words. Radel listened with interest, but still he wasn't convinced. He said, trying to assess what these spies, already condemned to death, might be able to offer him that wouldn't endanger him. 'But what can *you* offer *me*?' he sneered.

Lofty was ready with her answer. She turned her back on him, momentarily lowered her trousers and reached inside her vulva where she had hidden it, the last of the pearl necklace she had once worn in what now seemed another world, the day she had been presented to the Queen at Buckingham Palace. She rubbed it dry and held it up so that he could see it clearly in the weak

43

light of the candle.

Radel's eyes glistened. 'What is it?' he asked and before she could answer, he added, 'How valuable is it?'

'*Viel Geld*,' Lisa answered hastily. '*Eine Konigin hat es einmal gestragen.*'

Long-time communist that he was, Radel was impressed by the information, lie though it was, that the pearl had once been worn by the English queen. '*Tat sachlich*,' he said, licking suddenly dry lips, forgetting that by doing so he was revealing his ruined mouth to these foreign women, who were obviously very rich. 'But the men?'

Lisa beat him to it. 'We know where the men we want can be found.'

'Where?'

'The SS brothel. No, we don't mean those SS swine. We mean those Swedish sailors who frequent the place now.'

Radel looked puzzled. 'Why the Swedes? They're worse than the SS. They drink all the time. They'd be no use in bed...'

'Don't mess about.' Rosie, as bold as ever, cut him short. 'We have our reasons. Can you arrange what we want with the Swedes?'

Lisa translated hastily. Radel looked doubtful. Watching him carefully in the flickering yellow light, Lofty reached her hand down to the instep of her wooden clog. She touched the cold sharpness of the blade she kept hidden there. She had managed to hide it through a succession of camps. Her captors had probably never imagined that a woman would try to conceal the blade of a cut-throat razor. But she had, and she had sworn to herself that if the worst came to the worst, she'd slit her own wrists with it. Now she told herself that if Radel made one single suspicious move it would be his throat that would be slit and he'd never leave the *barracke* alive.

But Radel, the one-time ardent communist, had his own plans for the future. He knew *he*'d survive the camps. But when he did, the fate of the 'working masses' would no longer worry him. He wanted to be rich, have his ruined mouth fixed, wear fine suits and enjoy the favours of beautiful women, all the things that only money could buy. Karl Radel would become a capitalist. So he said, 'I'll do what you wish. I'll find your Swedes. But there'll be an additional price.' He smirked and this time he didn't mind showing his mouth.

Lisa translated and Lofty asked, 'What price? What do you want? We have nothing else.'

Radel continued to smirk. 'Oh yes, you

have.' He ran his other hand along the length of the ugly bull's pizzle as if the gesture had some special significance. 'The woman that those SS pigs called *"Titten".*'

Rosie's German was limited. All the same she recognized the SS men's nickname for her on account of her splendid breasts. She flushed angrily. She opened her mouth to tell the ugly little *Kapo* to go to hell, but Lofty beat her to it. 'Shut up,' she hissed. 'We'll promise anything to get out of this hellhole while we've still got a chance, Rosie.' She winked. 'But there's many a slip between the cup and lip, dear, as my old mother used to say.' She nodded to a waiting Lisa, who was grave and tense, for she had never been able to appreciate what the English thought was their tremendous sense of humour.

'We'll see about that when you have found us our Swede,' Lisa said in German.

Radel's smirk grew even larger. 'Good,' he said and, taking one last look at Rosie's remarkable breasts, he slunk through the door of the *barracke*, swinging his bull's pizzle happily, as if it were his own that he was holding in his dirty paw.

When they were sure he was out of earshot, Lofty said, 'I think that's one gentleman who is going to be sorely disappointed once he's done what he's supposed to do for us.'

'You can say that again,' Rosie said bitterly. 'I'm nae gonna let that creep maul my parts.'

There was a murmur of 'goodnight' and 'sleep tight'. Huddling together like passionate lovers so as not to lose precious body warmth in the freezing wooden hut, one by one they fell into an uneasy sleep, save for Lofty. For she, more than the rest, knew they were committed. How it would all work out, she didn't know. All she did know was that it would involve treachery and double treachery and, in the end, cold-blooded murder.

Three

The women had virtually pulled it off forty-eight hours later. It was midday. Twelve o'clock in the great sprawling camp was when the whole world revolved around half a litre of thin soup, made from meatless bones and whatever else the 'kitchen bulls' could find to fill out *die Mittagssuppe*. Now, for as long as it lasted, this canteen of thin lukewarm liquid was more important than loyalty to one's country, love, even God.

In the great rush for the huge kettles that contained the prisoners' main meal of the day, no one noticed Lisa as she got dangerously close to the wire. Why should they? The guards were enjoying the customary midday spectacle of these human skeletons in their clumsy wooden shoes hurrying across the parade ground, getting stuck in the mud, losing their sabots, fighting and cursing those who attempted to get in front of them. Why, this was even funnier than the

*Dick und Doof** comedy movies they showed in the SS cinema.

Lisa spotted the Swede. He was a great bear of a man, muffled up in a thick winter jacket complete with a fur collar. For a moment she envied him the warm coat, but then she saw he was finding his warmth in the bottle of schnapps he held in his big paw. He smiled in that silly way of a drunk and for a moment Lisa prayed he was not going to let them down. But she realized there was no time to consider that awful possibility. It would be only a matter of moments before the guards in the stork-legged watchtowers that lined the wire would tire of the watching skeletal wretches fight for the soup and return to their duties. Then it would take only one bored trigger-happy guard to press the trigger of his MG-42 and she'd be dead.

Hastily she withdrew the little leather bag made from the sole of a battered shoe they had taken from a dead inmate the night before and hefted it in her skinny, dirty hand to test its weight. She drew a breath and in that same instant tossed it over the wire. The Swede caught it neatly, raised his

*'*Fat and Daft*', the German name for Laurel and Hardy.

49

bottle as if in salute and then went on his somewhat unsteady way back to his ship down at the docks below.

Lisa let her shoulders slump in relief. It was done. The Swede had his message, plus the bribe made up from the bits and pieces that they had stolen from the previous night's corpses before the SS looters had been able to get at them. It had been a terrible, macabre, heartbreaking task searching those bags of bone for whatever treasure they had been able to conceal in the orifices of their emaciated bodies, but Lofty had insisted that they had to continue, even when some of the girls had begun to cry and sob. She had snapped at them almost angrily, 'Don't be silly, the lot of you. They're dead. We're alive. But if you're not so bloody foolish now, their death might mean we remain alive. Now ruddy well get on with it!' And so saying she had turned over the corpse of a bearded old man and had commenced searching his rectum for whatever he might have concealed there.

But there was still one more obstacle facing the women prisoners: the greedy little *Kapo*, Radel. They had all agreed that once he had had his way with Rosie, he would betray them one way or another. As Lisa said, 'The whole German nation is corrupt.

You can't trust any one of them. They are either Nazi, opportunist, or so scared of the Gestapo that they'd sell their own mothers to the authorities in order to save their own skins.'

Lofty had nodded her agreement and said in a solemn voice, 'There's only one way we can deal with the little bugger, girls, and you know that.' She hadn't spelled out what that way was, but she hadn't needed to; they knew already. By the time the huge camp at the edge of the frozen inland sea was settling down for yet another miserable night, they had made their plans on how to deal with the *Kapo*.

Radel had picked the *Kapos'* latrine for his rendezvous with *'Titten'*. It was not the normal place for a session of love-making, but in that death camp nothing was normal. Here at least, Radel must have thought when he chose the meeting place, he would be undisturbed. The SS would not deign to place their precious bottoms on the wooden boards soiled by contact with the 'skinny arses of the red commie pack'. As for the inmates, whose 'toilet' consisted of a trough without seats or water or any kind of cover where they squatted in rows, men and women mingled together, they wouldn't have dared to venture within twenty

51

minutes of the place where the notoriously evil-tempered *Kapos* carried out their bodily functions under a corrugated tin roof and behind a hessian screen.

Radel's choice of meeting place met with the approval of the women prisoners. As Lofty had explained, 'It's right up our street, girls. The SS will be in their brothel. The prisoners, poor devils, will be in their freezing huts for the night, and the *Kapos*'ll be getting pie-eyed on that illicit potato schnapps that they make with *our* potato ration, the bastards. So I think we can sort out our friend Radel undisturbed and at our leisure.' She smiled, but it was not a very pleasant one.

Squatting opposite her on a wooden bunk in the icy *barracke*, Rosie snapped, 'Not so much of yon leisure. I'm not having yon wee German rat fondling my breasts for over-long, Lofty.' And she had folded her arms across her splendid bosom as if prepared to defend her breasts to the very end.

'Don't you worry, Rosie,' Lofty had sooth-ed her. 'Friend Radel won't be touching your breasts – or those of any other woman for that matter – for very much longer.' She looked around the circle of faces. 'We agree then, do we, that Radel must die and dis-appear?' She hesitated only a fraction of a second. 'And you all know how he has to disappear, don't you...?' Her voice trailed away to nothing and a heavy silence descended upon the hut, broken only by the orders of the guard commander as he changed the SS guard on the wire, and, far away in the distance, the rumble of the permanent barrage that indicated the Russians were still attacking.

Radel had been ordered by the head *Kapo* to deal with one of the Russian prisoners. He was accused of stealing the smoke from the head *Kapo's* cigarette. This was a very serious crime and the head *Kapo*, a former communist schoolteacher from Berlin-Wedding, wanted it punished to the full. As he had told Radel in that prissy school-teacher's manner of his, 'These damned Ivans don't deserve communism. Unlike Germans, they have no idea of discipline and the communal good. They're a rabble of peasants. Comrade Stalin should have liquidated the whole damn bunch of them.'

Radel had agreed. He knew that most of the camp's inmates would have sold their soul for a smoke. They made 'tobacco' from virtually everything – weeds snatched from the fields when they were outside on work-ing parties, tea leaves stolen from the SS kitchens, anything. But the Russian prisoners were the worst. They seemed to spend all their time, when they were not hunting cats and rats for food, dreaming up cunning ideas for getting a free smoke.

This one, a big, cross-eyed fellow with a set of ugly teeth made of stainless steel, had picked on the wrong person. He had sauntered up to the chief *Kapo* with what looked like one of their coarse cigarettes made of newspaper stuck between his lips. Cheekily, he had asked for a light from the *Kapo*'s glowing cigarette end. The latter had been so surprised by the cross-eyed Russian's boldness that he had not had time to refuse. The next moment the Russian had touched the empty tube of newspaper to the *Kapo*'s cigarette and drawn in a huge breath, sucking up a lungful of the *Kapo*'s precious smoke. Naturally the *Kapo* had had him beaten into unconsciousness on the very spot. But now he wanted more; he wanted Radel to make an example of the Russian 'smoke thief'.

That night Radel was more concerned with getting his dirty paws on the English miss's big tits and then, when he had excited himself enough with them, getting down to some more serious action. Besides, he had never danced the mattress polka with an

English capitalist; it would be an additional thrill, he told himself as he faced the sulky Russian, his face swollen almost beyond recognition.

'Speak German?' he demanded.

'*Da*,' the Russian smoke thief answered.

'Good,' Radel said, swinging his bull's pizzle threateningly 'How say you? Guilty or not guilty?'

The Russian looked puzzled.

The *Kapo* didn't hesitate for a moment. He lashed out with the bull's pizzle. The Russian yelled. He reeled back, blood spurting in a bright-red arc from his shattered nose. 'Answer,' the *Kapo* demanded.

Still the Russian looked puzzled as he held his shattered nose, the blood seeping through his clasped fingers. Perhaps he didn't understand the question in German; perhaps he was one of those bull-headed Russians who were too stubborn to respond even when their life depended upon it. Radel didn't know, nor did he care. He was sick of the Russian. He wanted to get his hands on the Englishwoman's tits, squeeze the soft puddings, play with her nipples – they were large, he had seen that through the thin material of her prison uniform, and he liked large nipples. He had no more time to waste. His dirty hand fell to the knife that all the *Kapos* carried to defend themselves. His eyes narrowed.

Suddenly the Russian became aware of his danger. '*Njet*,' he choked urgently. '*Njet, tovarich*.' Hastily he reached inside his rags. He pulled out what looked like a badge, bright and shining, as if he treasured it, had kept it polished and clean when everything else about him was ragged and dirty. '*Kosomol*,' he croaked urgently.

Radel understood. The Russian was indicating that he was a member of the Soviet Youth Organization. He thought rightly that all the *Kapos* were communists and that this would save him, but the prisoner was wrong. Like all his fellow *Kapos* Radel hated the Russians as much as the SS did. The Russians were a dirty, inferior people, a third-class race that caused only trouble. He prodded the terrified Russian with his knife. 'Out!' he cried. '*Davoi ... Raus!*'

The Russian obeyed at once. Outside it was freezing. The camp looked almost beautiful in the sparkling brilliant-white of the hoar frost. But both the prisoner and his jailer had no eyes for the beauty of the night scene. The cold was too intense. It seemed to strike Radel a physical blow across the face. He gasped. He hoped the English lady was as hot as she looked. He'd need all the additional warmth he could get in the cold latrine.

Now he turned to the Russian. 'Run,' he cried, 'or freeze to death. *Boshe moi*,' he cursed in Russian. 'Run, you bastard ... Run!'

Suddenly the Russian broke into a lumbering run, hampered by the clumsy wooden shoes he was wearing. Radel ducked back into the cover of his hut. He knew what was going to happen now. And it did.

Abruptly the searchlights along the wire burst into light. Icy fingers of white light poked apart the darkness. They swept from left to right, seeking for the running man. The Russian quickly became aware of his danger. He started to zig-zag from side to side, running back towards the huts, slipping and sliding on the slick ground as he did so. Relentlessly the searchlights followed him. He was cornered. He faltered to a stop. He raised his hands. *'Nix schiessen,'* he cried in broken German. *'Bitte nix schiessen!'*

To no avail. The machine-gunners in their towers showed no mercy. Perhaps they were only too glad to move, to alter their frozen positions. They opened up from all sides. The Russian, blinded by the harsh white light, didn't stand a chance. Bullets slammed into him. He was whirled round and round like a crazy spinning top. Blood spurted from his holed body as if from a sieve until a harsh voice cried, '*Feuer einstellen ... Feuer einstellen!*'

The rattle of machine guns faltered. A few shots more and then it ceased altogether. Radel took one last look at the crumpled body lying in a red star of its blood. Then he hurried inside, warming himself with the thought of what was soon to come...

Four

Winston Churchill received Fleming in his bathroom. He wallowed in the old-fashioned bath, smoking a large cigar, with a glass of whisky on one side and his false teeth in another glass at the opposite end.

Standing around the bath was a valet who was warming a holed silk vest, an admiral, whom Fleming didn't know, and an elderly, bent civilian who the commander thought was vaguely familiar, though he couldn't place him at that particular moment. Not that he was worried. He was too fascinated by the sight of the naked head of the British Empire, immersed in grey water, like a glowing pink toothless Buddha.

Churchill caught the young naval officer's look and said cheerfully, 'Don't let me disconcert you, Commander. Last year my good friend President Roosevelt saw me in the White House in the altogether. He was embarrassed and was prepared to withdraw, but I said to the President, "Mr President, don't. You can see that the King's First Minister has nothing to hide from you.'" He looked down at his hairless body as if he might have had second thoughts and was wondering if he had something to hide after all. The bent elderly man in the grey suit flecked with dandruff, who in the years to come would be written about as 'M', stirred slightly.

Churchill got the hint. He said, 'Commander, let us get down to business. I will hide nothing from you either. Right from the start, I shall tell you that the mission I am going to entrust to your Thirty Commando is fraught with danger. Some of your chaps won't come back, I'm sure of that.' He reached for his whisky and took a sip, looking suddenly very thoughtful. 'But tell me a little about your Thirty Commando, I pray you.'

Swiftly Fleming launched into the speech that he had given so many times before when he had been trying to convince the powers that be of the need for a special commando.

Churchill listened attentively – for him. Opposite, the grey-haired, grey-suited civilian had frozen into inactivity again, hardly seeming to breathe, so that he might well have been dead.

Finally Fleming was finished and Churchill waited till the sergeant of the guard had relieved the Coldstream Guardsman in the garden and they had marched off, boots crisp and sharp on the gravel path this cold spring morning. Then he said, 'You have done well for yourself, Commander. A whole commando under command at your age. You'll go somewhere, my boy, I'm sure.'

Cynical as he was, Fleming couldn't help but blush. The old man, fat, naked and toothless, had seen through him right away. Perhaps that was why Churchill was so great. He knew how to cut through the crap. Churchill didn't seem to notice. As the valet indicated that his vest was warm enough to be put on, he allowed the admiral to hand him a large fluffy white towel and, rising from the water like a mini hippo, he started to dry himself, still puffing cheerfully at his cigar.

Chewing the cigar from one side of his toothless mouth to the other, Churchill said, 'The Hun is getting desperate. We can expect a lot of underhand tricks from him before he is finished. Not only Herr Hitler's secret weapons, perhaps gas and biological stuff, but also some sort of action against the hundred and fifty thousand British POWs in German hands. Perhaps blackmail, for all of them are under threat of death. You have heard of the death of some fifty-odd of our fine RAF pilots who escaped from their camp in Poland last year and have never been heard of since? We have reason to believe that they have been murdered by the Hun Gestapo. Then there are what the Hun calls the *Prominenz* – the prominent ones, you understand.'

Fleming did. He was proud of the German he had learned in Switzerland before the war. 'I understand, sir.' He stopped short, realizing that Churchill was listening only to himself; he always did when he was in full flow.

Churchill lowered his tone. He looked very serious now. 'The Hun will do something else, Fleming, something boundlessly evil, I'm afraid.' He hesitated, almost as if he couldn't bring himself to explain this 'boundless evil'. 'It is the women of the SOE. Nearly a dozen of these brave women, mostly radio operators for the various British underground circuits in France working with the French Resistance, were captured last autumn in that country. Two at least were put to death by the Hun on the spot. The others survived, being moved from camp to camp by the retreating Germans. Now we have reason to believe that

62

these survivors are located on the German coast in or around East Prussia.' He looked at the grey man, whose face, unlike Churchill's, revealed no concern for the women – perhaps because they were part of an organization that rivalled his own. 'C?'

When he spoke, C, who Fleming now realized was the mysterious head of the Special Intelligence Service, sometimes known as MI6, his dry, cracked voice revealed no emotion whatsoever. He said, 'We have received a communication from our Passport Control Officer in Stockholm.' He meant the SIS's representative in the Swedish capital, for the secret organization always used the passport control office as a diplomatic cover for its agents. 'One of his contacts, a seaman on a freighter plying between the East Prussian and Pomeranian ports on the Baltic, has given information about the presence of the missing women agents—'

'We know where they are,' Churchill broke in, as if he could no longer stand the slow, deliberate pace of the head of the SIS. 'We know, too, that these ladies suspect that they are to be put to death as part of the Hun's attempts to cover up the terrible things they have been doing in those death camps of theirs.' Churchill's voice hardened. 'We are not going to let anything happen to those brave ladies, who have risked all for their country.' There was steel in Churchill's tone now. 'Cost what it may, Commander, we must make an attempt to rescue them before it is too late. You understand?'

Fleming nodded, though he didn't really understand. His 30th Commando was not geared up for that kind of action. Yet as he tried to find some way of conveying this to the Prime Minister without appearing not to want the mission, he realized, too, that this was an opportunity for him to make a name for himself at last. Throughout the war he had always played second fiddle to whoever had been in charge of Naval Intelligence. In essence he had been a pen-pusher, sailing a desk. He had achieved no glory and had won no medals. Soon he'd be out of the navy and back in Fleet Street doing a hack job. It wasn't the role he envisaged for himself now that he was in his thirties. But if his Commando could pull off this daring rescue job, he'd get the headlines he lusted after; perhaps a good gong and then people, important people, would know who he was.

Bewildered as he was by the ramifications of this mission that had been thrust upon him so surprisingly, he forced himself to look eager, enthusiastic, saying, 'I am sure my chaps would be only too glad to rescue these ... er ... ladies, sir. In fact, although it's not our line of business, we'd deem it an honour.'

Churchill did not appear to be listening. Waving the admiral away haughtily, he beckoned the valet to come closer, bending his head like a child in a nursery so that the servant could pull the tattered vest over his head. He did so and then Churchill started puffing at his cigar again, while the four of them stood there, faces solemn, though Fleming, for his part, had never seen such a comical sight: the head of the British Empire in a vest that was too short for him, cigar clasped between his toothless gums.

Finally the Prime Minister waved his pudgy hand in dismissal, saying, 'You gentlemen will take care of the commander. Brief him well.' He gave Fleming a parting glance, as though seeing him for the first time. 'Don't let me down, Fleming. The safety of those brave women is very dear to me, remember that.' Abruptly Fleming realized that Winston Churchill was not just a comic figure; he was a dangerous man to cross, too. For all the Prime Minister's outrageous posturing, it would not be wise to get on the wrong side of him.

In the ante-room, the grey man, as Fleming now thought of the head of the SIS, mopped his damp brow and snapped angrily, 'The PM is absolutely impossible. He expects us to stand round while he carries out his ablutions as if we were a bunch of damned flunkeys.' He sat down on the hard stool.

The admiral, who looked decidedly out of place in these surroundings, said nothing. Instead he went to the set of wall charts, selected one and pulled it out. He rapped the map with his knuckles and said, 'The Baltic.'

C muttered something under his breath. Fleming thought he'd said, 'Like a bunch of damned schoolboys,' but he couldn't be certain. Instead he stared at the map, which was a rash of blue, red and black marks, stretching from one end of the inland sea to the other. 'The black chinograph is the Russians,' he announced, 'Coming in from the east in three prongs, along the coast and to the north and south of Berlin.' He looked at C, as if he expected the latter to make some comment. He didn't. His eyes were cold and unfeeling. They were the eyes of a man who regarded his fellow men as pawns to be dealt with – and dispensed with – when he felt they had outlived their usefulness or had become dangerous. At that moment it came to Fleming suddenly, startlingly, with the one hundred per cent certainty of a vision. C was not one bit interested in saving the women from the rival Intelligence service. Indeed, it seemed to the younger officer at that moment that C would be only too glad if they weren't saved from their terrible fate at all.

But Fleming had no time to dwell on that realization, for the admiral continued talking. 'The blue marks are those of the German positions along the Baltic coast and including most of the Baltic ports, large and small, from Konigsberg to Swinemunde, and then over on the other side in Schleswig-Holstein – here. I don't need to tell you, Commander, the red are the British positions on the line of the Rivers Elbe and Weser, where your own commando is waiting to join the advance.' Fleming nodded.

'So we might say,' the admiral went on, 'that we are engaged in something of a three-sided battle.'

'*Three*-sided battle?' Fleming queried hastily.

C beat the admiral to it. 'Yes, on the face of it we're fighting the Germans in the Baltic. But there's more to it than that, Fleming, and please remember this during

67

whatever is to come. Not only are we engaged against the Hun there, but, unknown to the world, we are also fighting the Russians. The Bolsheviks are our real enemies now. Their aim is to capture the exit to the Baltic before we can reach the coast at Lubeck – there. If we don't reach Lubeck in time they will sweep by us and be out into Denmark and the entrance to the North Sea. If they can do that, God forbid what might happen to these islands in the new battle to come!'

Suddenly Fleming felt an icy finger of fear trace its way down his spine. He shivered. He realized abruptly that this mission Churchill had just given him was not going to be as simple as it seemed. There were other forces at work, ones that he had not imagined till now. His thoughts of fame and instant glory vanished as swiftly as they had come, as the admiral said, 'Now, Fleming, about these skimmers we are going to give you for this op...'

Five

The women smelled them before they saw them. They gave off a nauseating stench, which reminded Lofty of the monkey house at Whipsnade Zoo before the war. Then, as the women watched in total silence from the window of the *barracke*, the first of the great column of ragged prisoners came into view. They were like skeletons. They stumbled and staggered, their breath fogging the icy air in a thick grey mist. Here and there a *Kapo* cracked a whip across their backs, but they did not even seem to notice the cruel lash; they were too far gone.

Some, however, retained hatred for their torturers. Although their skull-like faces were like death, their bulging eyes burnt with hatred for the German *Kapos* and their SS masters. Not that the SS, all mounted on little Siberian ponies, minded – or even noticed. Armed with pistols and sub-machine guns instead of whips, they yelled '*Los*', the command that the women had come to hate with a passion, and when some of the wretches fell behind or to the ground, the SS didn't hesitate. Not even dismounting, they leaned forward in the saddles of their shaggy ponies and ripped the victim's back open with a burst of automatic fire or blew the back of the prisoner's head off with a well-directed shot.

'Holy mother of God!' Rosie breathed, hands flying to her mouth in horror. 'How can men be so cruel to one another?'

It was a question that none of the horrified women could answer. Fat Otto, for his part, took it all in his stride. He took a swig of schnapps from his 'flatman', which these days he carried with him all the time, ever more nervous since he had learned that once he and his troop had been relieved of guard duty, they would be sent to the Front. He said thickly, for already he was quite drunk, 'Perhaps it's all for the best, ladies ... For the stiffs, I mean.'

Lofty, more alert to the gross NCO's words than the others, for she knew that their fate might well depend upon how she interpreted the SS pig's words, said, 'What do you mean?'

But, as drunk as he was, Fat Otto wasn't going to be drawn. Instead he said merely, 'They will be sent by ship to Cuxhaven,

Travemunde, somewhere like that, *perhaps*.'

Lofty knew her German geography well enough and it gave her some sense of security to hear that the prisoners were being sent to the western seaports, where the Germans had to be more careful about what they did, especially as the advancing Western allies were now on their doorstep. But she didn't like that 'perhaps'. What did Fat Otto mean? 'Why, don't you think they'll get there, *Oberscharführer*?' she asked.

Again Fat Otto wasn't very forthcoming. He shrugged his fat shoulders. Instead of answering her question, the ex-Savoy pastry cook said, 'They have found that communist swine Radel, the *Kapo*.'

She and the others froze at the mention of the man they had murdered so brutally two weeks before. She played stupid. 'Radel?'

Fat Otto took another swig at his *flatman*. 'You know, ladies, the one who was always trying to see you misses without clothes.' He chuckled. 'Why, I know not. You are all very thin. In our club the ladies are all very ... He made the gesture of outlining a very generous bosom and then rubbed his pudgy hands as if he were back in his old profession, kneading dough. He chuckled again. 'The *Kapos* do not like it – Radel being killed so. They want revenge. But these communists – swine that they are – stick together. Now, gracious miss,' he addressed Lofty whom he regarded as the leader of the women, 'make sure you are ready to move. Pack your things, eh!'

'Pack our things!' Rosie snorted angrily. 'What ruddy things?' She ran her hands down the shabby pyjamas, the only clothes she possessed in the world. Now she didn't even have a pair of knickers to wear. 'Perhaps I should wear a ballgown instead of this?'

Fat Otto was too drunk to be angry. He held up both hands, palms outwards to ward off the irate Scottish girl. 'Please, I carry out orders, only.'

Lofty told herself that was what they all said. No doubt they'd be doing the same when the Germans were brought to trial after the war, if she and the girls survived to see that eventuality.

Fat Otto clicked to attention and gave one of his sloppy salutes. 'Now I must go, ladies.' Then he was gone, stepping delicately, if slightly drunkenly, over a body with a shattered skull that lay in his path.

As always they waited in silence until the SS NCO was out of earshot before speaking. Then Lisa said, 'Things are going wrong.' As always Lisa was deliberate, seeing things in black and white.

Hastily Lofty stepped in. She knew that the mood of her fellow prisoners was fragile at the best of times. They had suffered so much since their capture, living on their nerves day in, day out. They could only take so much. 'No, Lisa, they're not.'

'But you heard what that fat pig said about the *Kapos*,' Nellie Dean objected. 'They'll show no mercy if they ever find out what we did to...' Her voice trailed away to nothing.

For a moment Lofty remembered that terrible scene, which she had tried to black out of her mind. If she didn't she felt she might well go mad with the horror of it all. They had been waiting for him, all of them armed with makeshift clubs. He'd entered the latrine – so dark that they could only mark his position because he had washed himself with proper perfumed soap – calling softly, 'Miss ... English Miss...' and then, more crudely, *'Titten, Fraulein Titten.'*

'Here,' Rosie had squeaked as ordered. *'Ich warte auf dich.'*

'Ich komme,' he had answered, his voice suddenly thick with lust.

He had moved forward hurriedly to stumble over Lofty's outstretched foot, sprawling full-length along the duckboards. They hadn't hesitated. They knew they daren't.

They had commenced beating him with the clubs, smashing a great blow against the back of his shaven skull so that he had lapsed into semi-consciousness and could not cry out.

Then they had done it. They had already removed the seating of a section of eight of the earth closets. Now they had carried him bodily towards the opening, trying to overcome the nauseating stench that came from the white maggot-riddled yellow mess below. They had not hesitated. On a soft command from Lofty they had dropped the stunned *Kapo* into the mess, praying that he would sink and choke to death at once while he was not conscious.

But to their horror he had not. The shock had awoken him. Spluttering and choking, trying to keep his head above that ghastly yellow mess, he had called, '*Please ... please ... nicht mehr ... nicht schlagen...*'

The fact that he had still been able to appeal to them, to talk, had infuriated the women. They were seized by a kind of primeval fury. Crying obscenities, they had smashed their makeshift clubs on to his head and shoulders. Bone splintered, a gleaming white against the scarlet flow of his blood. Desperately he had fought to hang on to the side of that nauseating cesspit. Rosie had shrieked, 'Make him let go of it ... Hit the bastard's hand!'

Nellie Dean had reacted immediately. Teeth bared like those of a predatory animal, she had aimed a tremendous blow at Radel's hand. His scream of absolute agony had been cut off as his lower face sank beneath that horrible mire. 'Drown, you bastard!' she had grunted, launching yet another tremendous blow at the hand. The bones had splintered like matchwood. That had done it. The shattered hand relaxed its hold. Next moment Radel's head had disappeared beneath the ordure. A few bubbles and then the surface became calm. Radel had died.

Now Lofty shrugged off that terrible memory. She knew that as long as she lived, she would never forget the horrible murder, the kind of deed she had never suspected women might be capable of. In France she had shot a German soldier outside Orleans. But he had been armed and some distance away from her. In a way that had been a clean death ... She forced herself to stop dwelling on the matter and said, her voice clearly under control again, 'All right, girls, we know the dangers. But the *Kapos* have got to tumble to us first, and I think we'll have to be out of here before then. Our concern must be the next twenty-four hours or so. So let's see what we can pack, as our fat friend has ordered to do. Come on.'

That long, grey April day, it was clear that the camp was being emptied – and rapidly. There were no work details. Instead the poor wretches of inmates were being taken out in their hundreds by the sour-faced *Kapos* and marched to an assembly point near the main gate with its mocking inscription above it: *Arbeit Macht Frei**.

From there, carrying their pathetic bits and pieces and clutching half a loaf of hard Army bread, their ration for the day, they were marched off to the coast below. Those who couldn't march were shot on the spot by the SS guards, to be cleared away by the next group at the assembly point.

Every now and again as the women stowed their own bits and pieces, they broke off to ask Lofty that one overwhelming question – one that she found impossible to answer. Had the bribed Swedish sailor delivered their message to the nearest British consul in his homeland? The first time Nellie posed the question, Lofty could have screamed. 'How the hell do *I* know, Nellie!' But she didn't. She knew the women's nerves were

* 'Works Frees'.

76

stretched to the limit. They needed reassurance. So she lied the best she could, telling them throughout that long day while the camp was being evacuated, 'These things take a long time, girls, and you can be sure General Gubbins,' she meant the head of the SOE organization, 'won't abandon us. No sir!' But even as she lied to her fellow prisoners, she knew that in the confusion and chaos of this breakdown of German organization, anything could happen; there were no certainties.

But as the day wore on, Lofty became aware that there was at least one certainty. The Russians to the east were coming ever closer. Now the women could hear the boom of Russian artillery quite clearly, and it was not only heavy guns that they could hear, but also those of a smaller calibre. Not only that but they could also make out the work of Wehrmacht wrecking crews, carrying out Hitler's 'Operation Nero', leaving nothing behind to the enemy but scorched earth. Everywhere to the east they could see the flames as villages were ignited and factories were blown up. It was clear that the German Army was in full retreat.

Seeing the destruction to the east and knowing it wouldn't be long before the Red Army fought its way to the camp and the coast beyond, Lofty considered a new plan of escape. They could hide out in the deserted camp until the Russians came. She had no idea what they would live on and how long they could survive on the few scraps of bone-hard bread they had managed to save. She knew they might well be able to escape discovery until the arrival of the Red Army. But how safe would they be from their potential 'liberators'? She had heard all the terrible tales of how the Russians had behaved in 'liberated' German territory: the mass rapes, shootings, crucifixion of German pastors to the doors of their own churches and the like. Would they treat them, their British allies, any differently?

But before Lofty could decide, the decision was made for her. Zooming in at ground level, its prop wash lashing the trees below into a fury, a twin-engined plane with the roundels of the RAF painted on its wings ignored the flak that burst into frantic activity on all sides. The pilot seemed to bear a charmed life. He came through the angry flashes of cherry-red flame and bursts of grey smoke time and time again. Then, as Lofty cried excitedly, 'Girls, it's a Mosquito!' the pilot zoomed upwards. In that same instant a white banner floated from the rear of the fuselage. For one startled moment the entranced women couldn't believe the evidence of their own eyes. But clearly outlined against the white of the linen were three letters: SOE. They were the initials of their own secret organization. They had been discovered!

'Oh, girls,' Lofty said thickly, the tears already streaming down her cheeks. 'They haven't abandoned us ... The message got through!'

Above them the young pilot twisted his plane round in the victory roll and then he was gone, flying back to the west, his message safely delivered.

Six

Franco, the waiter who always served Fleming when he dined at Frascati's, beamed when he saw his favourite client enter the upper-class restaurant. The commander was a very fussy customer; he always knew better about the food than did the waiters. But he *was* a good tipper, and that was the main thing for the waiter, who said he was from St Tropez, though in reality he came from Sicily. '*Bonjour, mon commandant*,' he greeted Fleming, rubbing his greasy hands together, as if he were already savouring the fat tip Fleming would give him. 'I have something special for you today,' he continued in his fractured English. 'Garlic mushromps on buttered toast.' He beamed.

'Mushrooms,' Fleming corrected him routinely.

'*Oui*,' Franco said. 'Mushromps.'

Fleming gave up.

He passed the bowing waiter to where C was sitting, slumped in one of the place's faded plush chairs. He was staring out at the rain, his face set and as moody as ever. He might well have been dead. For a moment Fleming paused and stared at the head of the Secret Intelligence Service, wondering why he had been summoned to meet C here. The head of the SIS was usually to be found at White's, where he felt safe, surrounded by his cronies and friends from Eton and the Life Guards. Why meet in this somewhat flash place, where generals took their tarts and shady big businessmen did even shadier deals over French champagne at God knows how much a bottle? Fleming could only guess that C didn't want anyone of importance to see that he was dealing with someone from another intelligence service, especially Naval Intelligence. For a second or two he considered whether it was something to do with this new operation that had been proposed for his 30th Commando, though for the life of him he couldn't fathom why C should be particularly interested in the op – apart from giving his professional advice at the intelligence briefing. Then as Franco started to wipe the chalked menu off the blackboard, indicating that some of the place's lunch dishes would be off soon, he broke his reverie and hurried forwards; he didn't want to have to eat some of that bloody *snoek*, or whatever that South African stuff was called this particular afternoon.

'Sir?'

C took his time looking up at Fleming. He was obviously not a man to be hurried. Fleming, a product of Eton himself, realized that it was the old Etonian business of never appearing to be flustered, out of control 'Oh, it's you, Fleming,' C said, although he had long recognized the naval intelligence officer from his reflection in the big window opposite. 'Please sit down.'

'Thank you, sir.'

C pushed a menu towards him. 'Better order. There's never anything on the menu these days except those bloody dried eggs and some form of whale meat.'

'Yessir,' Fleming agreed dutifully, wondering if C could be so naive or short-sighted not to realize that all around him rich businessmen were eating the same kind of opulent menus, albeit black-market, as they had done before the war.

When the waiter had taken their order, C opened the conversation with, 'Not bad security here, I suppose, for a place of its kind.' Fleming, a snob himself, agreed with the sentiment. Frascati's was a bit on the louche side. 'Not packed in like sardines as one usually is in these foreign places.' C dropped the subject and for a few moments his grey face seemed almost animated. 'Some say the PM is an eighteenth-century man, Fleming,' he said, surprising the latter with this sudden change of direction. 'And in some ways he is. Rather like his ancestors, grandees, who didn't give a damn what people thought about them. Just like that meeting, him wandering around in the altogether, what?'

Fleming agreed.

'But there is that American streak in the PM, too. That "get up and go", as our cousins across the sea tend to call it.' There was no mistaking the contempt in his voice. 'Comes from his mother, I suppose. The PM is very modern in that way. He likes the publicity and the headlines.' He paused and let Franco put the 'mushromps' down in front of them, as if he were serving one of the world's greatest dishes. C touched one of the garlic mushrooms hesitantly with his fork, caught a whiff of the garlic, wrinkled his nose in evident distaste, and decided he didn't want Franco's celebrated 'mushromps'.

Reluctantly Fleming followed suit, resigning himself to whatever rubbish the restaurant would serve for the main meal, for it was obvious that C, as rich as he was, would not pay black-market prices for a decent meal.

'Now, Fleming,' C said, 'you obviously wonder why I've asked you here and what all this with the PM, etc, has got to do with your mission.'

Cautiously, Fleming said, 'Yessir, I suppose I do.'

'Well, it's like this, Fleming. Back in 'forty, when the PM set up the SOE, I and my associates were not too well pleased. It seemed to us that it was a reflection on our intelligence-gathering abilities – and I must admit we had made some bad mistakes in continental Europe before Dunkirk.' He frowned momentarily and his eyes seemed to disappear in a sea of facial wrinkles. 'No matter. Since then we've made up for it. We've contributed a great deal to the winning of this war.'

'Yessir. So I've heard.'

Opposite them a fat, middle-aged civilian dressed in an expensive suit, who obviously had his hand up the skirt of the brassy blonde, half his age, sitting with him, was crying at Franco, 'Come on, Franco, get your bloody finger out. Bring us some more bubbly. Only the best though.' He winked at the girl and obviously shoved his hand higher between her legs, for she jumped abruptly. 'Got to get my little darling in the right mood for you-know-what, sweetie.'

The brassy blonde giggled and C said, 'What dreadful people one has to mix with these days. God knows what society is going to be like after this show is over.' He tut-tutted.

Fleming looked sympathetic, though, upper-class as he was, he didn't give a damn about post-war society as long as he could make plenty of money out of it and be able to buy expensive *poules* like the brassy blonde, who was now obviously enjoying whatever the businessman was doing to her underneath the table.

'Now with the war virtually over, the PM will have to make a major decision as far as Intelligence is concerned, Fleming. There can't be two large-scale British intelligence agencies operating abroad in the post-war world. It's got to be either my SIS or General Gubbins' SOE. Got that?'

'Yessir.' Fleming certainly had. It was the old Whitehall power game that he had come to know all too well since joining Naval Intelligence. Dog eat dog. He didn't say the obvious thing that had come to his mind immediately. People like C didn't like what the former might call 'counter-jumpers' –

smart young fellows on the make who knew all the answers immediately. So he let C say it for him.

'It is quite clear then that one of the two organizations must go, and it is equally clear, Fleming, that it will not be my SIS that will be doing the departing. Clear?'

'Clear, sir.'

'So now we come to these unfortunate women prisoners of the Hun. If they are rescued and come back in a blaze of glory, you can be reassured that Gubbins will see to it that their story will feature in the headlines. You are a former newspaperman, Fleming. You know about these things. Gubbins has already leaked more than enough to the press. Now, what would that kind of publicity do for the PM? He'd lap it up. With the election coming up as soon as the war ends, you can see him savouring the publicity to the full – gongs at the Palace, radio interviews on the Home Service, newsreel stuff on Pathé in every cinema in the land...' He paused for breath, his wrinkled grey face flushed with the effort of so much talking.

Over at the table opposite, the businessman was obviously feeling the effects of the bubbly. He had lost all his inhibitions and it was quite clear what he was doing to the blonde beneath the table. Indeed she was now gasping open-mouthed, sprawling back in the chair, her legs spread. Fleming felt himself grow a little excited. He'd have a woman before this day was out, he told himself.

'So,' C was saying, 'what does all this amount to, Fleming? I shall tell you. Naturally I am in no position to order you to do what I wish. However, I can make it worth your while to help me. After all, you won't be staying in the Navy when this show is over, and I am sure I can help you get a new start in civilian life. I have the contacts.' He looked shrewdly at Fleming, as though assessing him for the first time.

Fleming forgot the drunken businessman and the panting blonde tart. After six years in the Navy he hadn't intended to go back to the dreary business of newspaper management. C, he knew, had contacts everywhere – *exciting* contacts. God, C might even want to recruit him into his own service as an agent. That would be the *real* adventure he had craved all throughout this long war. 'How can I help, sir?' he asked eagerly.

C lowered his voice, looking around in case he was overheard. 'These women. We know where they are now. We can also guess that they are soon going to be shipped across the Baltic. The time has come to rescue them, just in case the Hun has other plans for them. That is the PM's plan. But not mine.'

Fleming looked a little confused. C didn't seem to notice. He said, 'I feel we can't trust the Hun to do the job for us – the elimination of these women.'

Fleming felt icy fear trace its way down his spine. C was ruthless, he had always known that, ever since he had been recruited into Naval Intelligence, but up to now he hadn't realized just how ruthless the spymaster could be. In essence the head of the British Secret Intelligence Service was suggesting that several of his own countrywomen should be left to die in order to save his own service. All the same, Fleming, the opportunist, kept his feelings to himself; his lean, cynical face revealed nothing.

'So,' C said deliberately, *'we – you –* have to ensure that they are left to whatever fate has in store for them. You understand?'

'You mean, sir, that I am not to take this rescue bid ... er ... too seriously?'

'Something like that.'

Franco was approaching, bearing a covered silver tray, that Fleming had ordered off his own bat. It was venison ragout with wild mushrooms. It had cost the earth, but it would be worth it to gain C's favour and his contacts. C sniffed appreciatively. 'Now that smells better. Think we can obtain a good bottle to go with it, Fleming?'

'I'm sure that can be arranged, sir,' the latter answered as the brassy blonde swung out her hand and knocked over the ice bucket that contained the champagne.

C shook his grey head as a fawning Franco started to serve the ragout. 'Awful types one has to mix with these days, Fleming,' he commented. 'And that sort of chap over there will probably be putting down his son's name for the school, too, Fleming.' He shook his head again.

Fleming, his fellow old Etonian, did the same. 'Yessir, after this war Eton'll probably go to pot, too.'

'I fear so, Fleming,' the other man said, tasting the venison. 'There's a lack of morality about London these days. I blame it on the Yanks ... I say, Fleming, this ragout *is* good!'

Outside the old man who sold the *Evening Standard* was quavering his usual cracked voice, 'Monty ready to cross the Elbe River ... Monty ready to cross...' But the two old Etonians were not listening; they were too busy with their venison ragout. Besides,

89

Franco had produced a very good bottle of claret from Frascati's cellars and it wasn't every day that you could drink a bottle of Mouton in London in the spring of 1945, was it?

TWO

Captain Slaughter

One

A thin grey mist hung over the side arm of the River Elbe. It clung to the embankment in a wet gossamer. It deadened the sound of the guns in the far-off Hamburg area and lent a brooding, mysterious stillness to the scene as the commandos closed in, hugging the ditches and the verges so that they made no sound at all.

Despite the eerie quality of the dawn, with tension seemingly hanging in the very air, the young commando was enthusiastic – even happy. 'I say, sir,' he gushed sotto voce to Fleming who was huddled in his naval greatcoat. 'This is the stuff to give the troops – the real thing. It's all very well looking for that secret scientific stuff, but sometimes a chap needs a bit of real excitement, feels he's earning his pay, what, sir.' He ran the blade of his razor-sharp commando knife across his palm, as if he were already slitting the throat of some unsuspecting German sentry.

Fleming grunted something and wished he could light up one of his Bond Street specials, but he knew that was impossible, of course. That would give their position away to the Huns, who were less than two hundred yards or so to their immediate front.

Bill Williams, Monty's chief of intelligence, had informed him only six hours before that reconnaissance had discovered that a bridge still stood over the River Elbe after all. Up till then they had thought they had all been destroyed. Now they knew there was still a railway bridge intact opposite Lauenburg on the river. It would not be much use for vehicular traffic as yet – that would come when it was captured – but infantry such as his 30th Commando would be able to utilize it for a surprise crossing of the Elbe.

Indeed, Brigadier Williams and his chief, Montgomery, were so enthusiastic about the possible capture of the bridge at Lauenburg that they had already alerted a whole army corps to stand by to follow up the capture. Not that the possibility of a major assault on Germany's last natural barrier, the river, interested Fleming. For him the attack on the bridge was merely a feint so that he could get the two skimmers into the river and on their way up-river towards the sea.

By doing so he would accord with C's wishes and yet at the same time would seem to have carried out his part in the rescue of the SOE women. For, on consideration, he had realized it would be too dangerous to do more than go through the motions. Churchill would want to know why the rescue of the women had gone wrong and he wanted to come out of any such inquiry with a clean record. So the bridge would be assaulted, the skimmer crews would be able to get their secret craft into the river under the cover of the attack and everybody would be happy, whatever the outcome. Even before the balloon went up, Fleming was sure what that outcome would be: failure.

Now the NCOs were getting their men into position. In staggered platoons they'd approach the bridge using the ditches on both sides of the road that led from Luneburg to Lauenburg. Once they were close enough to the railway bridge, they'd use the embankment to the bridge's left to make their final rush.

As the eager young commando officer, who would lead the assault, had explained to Fleming earlier, 'We'll go in without any supporting fire, Commander. We don't want to alert old Jerry we're coming so that he can blow up the bridge's demolition charges. Once we've captured the far end of the structure—'

'*If*,' a cynical voice at the back of Fleming's brain had interjected. 'If, my friend!'

'Then we'll bring down interdiction fire to stop any enemy counter-attack and wait for the reinforcements to come up. It should be a piece of cake, sir,' he added with youthful enthusiasm. 'My chaps can't get started soon enough.'

'Good show,' Fleming had said, trying to ape the young officer's enthusiasm. 'I'm sure you've got it just right.'

Now Fleming waited in the pre-dawn cold as the commandos, in their green berets, checked their equipment for the last time, tapping their magazines to ensure they were firmly fixed, hitching up their small packs to more comfortable positions, urinating in a cloud of steam in the ditch and whispering supposed jokes to one another in the manner of men going into their first attack.

Fleming didn't feel for his men. For him they were working men in khaki uniform, working-class men, whose fate, he thought, was merely to be useful to those of his own class. Their thoughts, their emotions – if they had any – their feelings, even their very lives were of little importance to him. After all, they were simple creatures, happy with their 'char', their 'fags', their 'bully beef'. They'd do their duty, serve their purpose, and then die violently. More, he didn't expect of them.

To his right, kneeling on the cobbled road, the young officer and his senior NCOs were comparing the time, staring hard at the green-glowing dials of their watches. 'All right,' the officer was saying, using the time-honoured military joke on such tense occasions, 'circumcise your watches, men ... It's exactly zero five hundred hours.' The attack on the bridge at Lauenburg could commence. The rescue mission was under-way...

Captain Slaughter of the Special Boat Service swam easily, effortlessly. It was as if the big soldier was hardly aware that he was swimming in the fast-running water of the River Elbe. He breathed steadily and slowly, filling and emptying his lungs at regular intervals. He was aware that he must not use up the 'mix' in the container on his back, which fed the mask he wore, too quickly. Veteran that he was, he knew he might need a reserve, for as he always tried to impress upon his skimmer teams: 'Always expect the unexpected, for the unexpected always happens.' It was not surprising that some of the more bolshy of his skimmer teams called him 'Captain Unexpected' behind his back, for the big muscular soldier – veteran of the Med and the Normandy landings – was not a man to be trifled with. As his one-time boss, the Earl Jellico, had said of him after the disaster of Rhode when Slaughter had taken out ten German paras single-handed, armed only with a dud Eyetie pistol and a dozen rounds, 'Slaughter by name, Slaughter by nature!'

Now the light was turning greenish as it filtered down from the surface of the river. That indicated to the lone swimmer that it was approaching dawn, when the attack on the bridge at Lauenburg was scheduled to start. He flashed a glance at the wristwatch strapped next to his razor-sharp combat knife and then on to his underwater compass. He was dead on course and he had five minutes of swimming time left. Now the bridge would be immediately to his front. To his right was Artlenburg, where his men were waiting for his signal behind the windmill on the dyke, and opposite on the other side, held by the Germans, would be the red-brick *Gasthaus* that the enemy was using as their lookout post. Above it, at Geesthacht, were the dug-in German police battalion hurriedly dispatched from Hamburg to reinforce this new front.

Slaughter knew the odds were against him. But since he had first volunteered for the SBS back in '42, they always had been. He had learned to live with that fact. The key to survival was to know your job, keep your nerves steady and, as Jellico had phrased it more than once when the situation had become hairy, 'Maintain a tight sphincter.' Slaughter smiled at the memory and wondered for an instant where Jellico and the rest of the men with whom he had started out in '42 were now. Probably dead, he told himself, in that no-nonsense manner of his. Then he forgot his old comrades and concentrated on the job at hand. The water was getting darker. That indicated that he was getting closer to the shallows.

Suddenly he stopped swimming. Something was coming towards him. For a moment he thought it was a dead body, swaying gently, as if glimpsed at the bottom of a muddy pool. Next instant he saw it was an old Jerry greatcoat, swollen by the water, the empty sleeves flapping like grotesque arms. He swallowed hard, feeling a chump. A jerry greatcoat! Some poor sod, he told himself, ought to be on a fizzer for losing his greatcoat.

A few moments later he dismissed from his mind the greatcoat and the surprise it had caused. For directly ahead he glimpsed what Intelligence back at Monty's HQ had predicted when the skimmer teams had been briefed by the owlish, bespectacled ex-don, who was now Montgomery's chief of intelligence, Brigadier Williams.

It was the usual sort of obstacle that both sides used when trying to protect waterways: chain line, with dangling from it, at regular intervals, small grey tubes: mines. If the German defenders of the Elbe had still been using the waterway for their shipping, the chain line would have been left at the bottom of the river. Now that the British were obviously preparing to cross, and all but fast motorboats had stopped using the Elbe, the chain line had been pulled tight. Any unsuspecting British craft, a landing barge or DUKW, would be blown to pieces if it hit that chain.

Slaughter trod water and surveyed the simple but deadly device. His skimmers had a very shallow draught. Still, he couldn't risk leaving this section of the chain in place in case the swell from the fast-moving secret craft washed the chain line with its mines up higher. He realized that he'd have to take a section out – and do it fast before the attack

100

on the Lauenburg bridge ended. Once the fire fight had ceased, the noise he'd make would probably be heard all the way to Berlin.

'Balls!' he cursed to himself as he prepared to tackle the chain and its lethal mines. Like everything else of the plan worked out by that snobbish twerp, Fleming, with his expensive cologne and stupid ivory cigarette-holder, it entailed dangers at every stage – dangers that Fleming seemed to ignore. But then, Slaughter told himself as he started to cut the first tubular mine free from the chain, Fleming wasn't going to take part in this op. He'd be back in Whitehall most likely, nicely safe and sound, the affected prick...

A mile or so away, Fleming waited as the young commando officer loaded his Verey pistol. His nerves were tingling with excitement. Apart from the bombing of London, this was the closest he had come to action in six years of war. In a minute men would commence a battle in which some of them would die. He wished he'd brought his notebook with him. He could have made notes. Still, he'd impress this moment on his mind's eye so that he'd be able to use it later in his writing.

The young officer raised his pistol above

his head. He pressed the trigger. Crack! A soft plop. A hissing sound. Next moment the flare started to ascend into the dawn sky. Another crack, louder this time. The flare burst into a gaudy green flower of light. Below, their upturned faces were coloured an unnatural glowing hue. Then the commandos were hurrying forward, their small packs bouncing up and down on their backs, as if they couldn't go to their deaths swiftly enough. The rescue attempt had commenced...

Two

The commandos went forward in a rush. They knew that they had to turf out the German defenders of the bridge right from the start. The Germans were supposed to be mainly from the German Home Guard, the *Volkssturm* – 'old syphilitic pricks', as Monty's Intelligence officer had said. 'They are hidden behind six feet of concrete. Once they dig their heels in it'll be one helluva job trying to winkle them out of their positions.'

Now the men in the green berets swept up the verges to the embankment that ran along the railway line from Berlin to Hamburg and on to the bridge over the River Elbe. For a few moments their attack went silently, broken only by the sound of their own hectic breathing and the odd clink of a bayonet scabbard or the inevitable tin tea mug clattering against their small packs.

Then, with startling suddenness, though they had been expecting it all along, a star shell exploded over their heads. In an

103

instant they had been illuminated, a stark black against the harsh silver light. The defenders reacted. A stick grenade sailed over the top of the embankment, exploding in a burst of vicious cherry-red flame. A commando went down, clutching his ripped-open stomach, crying for his mother. Next to him, his comrade paused momentarily and loosed a savage salvo from his tommy gun. The man who had thrown the grenade reeled back, his hands holding his shattered face, moaning, *'Ich bin blind ... Blind ... helf' mir, Kameraden!'*

But no comrades were coming forward to help the blinded man. As the angry snap-and-crackle of the small arms battle grew in volume it was every man for himself. The aged defenders were sticking to the safety of their holes.

Carried away by the unreasoning blood-lust of battle, the young commando officer waved the claymore that he affected, crying, 'Rally on me, lads ... Come on, we've got 'em on the run. Come!' He slashed wildly at the figure that had just popped up from the embankment in front of him, brandishing a machine pistol. The German didn't have a chance to fire it. He screamed, high and hysterical, like a woman might, a great open wound carved in his face with what looked

104

like strawberry jam oozing from it. The attack went on.

Now the attackers were turning the enemy's flank. Over on the other side of the river, at Lauenburg, at the top of what looked like a cliff, a multiple flak gun had opened up. It was pumping a thousand shells a minute from its four cannon across the water in a lethal white-glowing morse. It looked as if the commandos were advancing into a solid wall of sudden death. But the gunners were firing high and the men in the green berets were used to advancing against live fire. They pressed home their attack, bent low like farm labourers ploughing through a muddy field under heavy rain.

Up front, still swinging his claymore wildly, the young commando officer breasted the embankment. To his right was the far end of the railway bridge. Beyond lay the station. He cheered. They were almost in sight of their objective. Behind him his men quickened their pace, ignoring the wild firing that was coming from the German defenders on the bridge itself. They seemed to be retreating, snapping off unaimed shots to left and right as they did so. 'They're cracking, lads!' the young officer cried above the racket. 'Up and at 'em! We've got 'em on the run...'

He never finished this exhortation. At that moment the railway bridge started to tremble and shake furiously. It was as if it were alive. A series of angry blue sparks ran its length. The stanchions overhead buckled and began to crumble. Little puffs of smoke appeared between the tracks. The commandos forgot the attack. They grabbed for support. The officer was pushed to his knees. His claymore tumbled from his hand. Even as he died, he knew the attack had failed. Then in one all-consuming, deafening roar, the centre of the bridge collapsed, taking with it both friend and foe. The German defenders had blown the bridge at Lauenburg.

Five minutes later, crouched in a ditch with a tarpaulin over his head, Fleming, his nose wrinkled in disgust at the earthy smell of the commando operator, who didn't seem to have washed for days, listened to the metallic distorted message coming over the crackling I8-set.

'Sunray ... Sunray ... Objective not taken ... Bridge blown ... Heavy casualties ... Pulling back ... Sunray ... Sunray...'

Fleming, who was 'Sunray', allowed himself a tight smile as the radio went and the commando operator slipped off the earphones and cursed, 'Christ Almighty, it

106

looks as if the lads have bought it this time, sir.'

'Yes, unfortunately,' Fleming replied without feeling. He stared out at the flames on the horizon and the crazy zig-zag of tracer as the German defenders continued to fire wildly in all directions. He told himself that the whole front would be alerted by now. For the time being, there would be no more attempts to cross the Elbe. He had done his little bit to put a spoke in the wheel of the rescue operation. C in London would be pleased with him, and he had kept his own hands clean. He couldn't help it that the Germans had blown the Lauenburg bridge before his commandos could seize it.

He raised himself cautiously from beneath the tarpaulin. He wasn't taking any chances. There were still plenty of crazy fanatical German kids in short pants wandering about behind British lines, taking potshots at lone British vehicles with their rocket-launchers and snipers' rifles. Fleming thought his life too precious to be terminated violently by some damnfool Hun Hitler Youth.

'Try to keep in contact, signaller,' he told the radio man. 'I'm taking the jeep back to GHQ. Clear?'

'Yessir,' the signaller answered smartly.

But to himself he said, 'Typical bloody toff. Goes and gets the lads slaughtered and then off back to HQ for bacon and eggs, more than likely. Not a frigging care in the frigging world.' He sniffed and told himself that he'd vote Labour like a shot once Winnie called a general election and then they'd get rid of upper-class twits like Commander Fleming for good.

With his drawn revolver on his lap and his Thompson sub-machine on the empty seat next to him, Fleming drove carefully through the dawn landscape, his gaze flicking from one verge to the other, ready to press down hard on the accelerator at the first sign of danger. But the wartorn landscape was strangely deserted, save for the odd shell hole and burned-out tank out in the fields, each vehicle surrounded by a little circle of crude crosses made of tree branches or upturned rifles, with helmets – German and British – hanging from them.

A little more relaxed, Fleming started to let his mind wander. So far things were going all right, but he was a little worried about Slaughter and his bunch of thugs. He hadn't liked the man right from the start. One could see that he was bolshy even from the way he wore his uniform, which was decidedly sloppy and not quite regulation.

The fact that Slaughter's chest bore the ribbon of the Military Medal in addition to the Military Cross also indicated that the big captain of the SBS had come up through the ranks. Probably, Fleming had told himself, he'd been one of those pushy regular NCOs who had used the war and the lack of officers to get himself commissioned.

Nor had Fleming liked Slaughter's reaction after he had detailed the rescue mission to him over the big map of the Baltic. When Fleming had finished, Slaughter had said straight out, without any beating about the bush, 'Why, Commander, a mission like that is bloody impossible – *absolutely*!'

It had been with difficulty that Fleming had kept his temper. The other man, with his crooked grin and tough, bronzed face, was not only insubordinate, he was damned insolent, too.

'Why is it impossible?' Fleming had asked, forcing himself to keep calm. After all, Churchill had suggested the use of Slaughter and his skimmers.

'Because there are too many imponderables, Commander, that's why.'

'What, for instance?'

Slaughter had tugged the end of his big tongue, as though considering whether it was worth his while going into the details; as if he might well be wasting his time on this office wallah. The sight made Fleming even more angry. But he controlled himself.

'Well, for example, the distances me and my chaps will have to cover with the skimmers. How are we going to manage to take them overland once we leave the Elbe at, say, Lenzen and head for the Baltic at Wismar. Then there's the upper Baltic. It's full of German shipping fleeing the Russians to the east. Finally, it'll be like looking for a needle in a hay-stack trying to find those SOE women among all those refugees and Jerry soldiers. And all the while, every hour of every day, we stand a good chance of being discovered.' He paused for breath and looked challengingly at Fleming.

Fleming lost his temper. 'Do you mean, Captain, that you are too afraid to undertake this mission? I am sure that if you are, your people in Poole will be able to provide me with some officer who is more willing to take a risk, what?'

Slaughter had clenched his fist, his jaw suddenly jutting out, and for a moment a worried Fleming thought he might well just lash out and hit him. He had heard the ugly rumours that the skimmer commander had been forced to volunteer for the SBS back in '42 in Egypt because he had struck his commanding officer in a fit of rage and it had been either the SBS or a court martial.

But Fleming had been wrong. Slaughter said, 'Of course I'll take on the job. What Englishman would allow those brave women, who have risked their lives behind enemy lines for their country, to be done to death without making the attempt at rescue. No! What I'm saying to you, Commander, is this: the plan is absolute bullshit. As it stands, we haven't got a chance of making it, and if we don't make it to the upper Baltic those women will die.'

'So what do you suggest, Captain?'

'Bribes.'

'Bribes?'

'Yes, of course. The Jerries are about at the end of their tether,' Slaughter retorted. 'Only the fools among them, like those Hitler Youth kids, don't realize they've lost the frigging war. The great majority of 'em do. But why should they help us, their enemies, unless they get something out of it?'

Fleming, the cynic whose enemies said he knew the price of everything, but the value of nothing, said, 'All right, I'll buy that. What kind of bribes?'

'The obvious – cigarettes. They're the only currency of any value in Germany today.

Then good-conduct certificates for their Jerries' bad boys. Something signed by an Allied officer stating that they've always been against the Führer and that they love Jews, that kind of bullshit. Gold coins, if we can get 'em. That's the stuff we'll need if we're going to buy our way through Germany, Fleming.'

Fleming had noticed that omission of his rank, but he hadn't commented upon it. He knew that he'd get his revenge on the cocky bastard one way or another. 'Yes, I can get you that sort of stuff, Slaughter, save for the gold coins. Anything else?'

Slaughter had looked at him for what Fleming thought was a long time, so much so that he had felt himself blushing – something he hadn't done since he got expelled from Eton. Then finally Slaughter had said, 'Yes. Full power to conduct this operation in any way I want.'

Now as he rattled along the cobbled road, routinely avoiding the shell crates as he did so, Fleming again felt the warm glow of satisfaction that he had granted the big thug's request. Slaughter had walked straight into a trap of his own making. When the second half of the op. failed as the first half had done, if anyone was going to be held responsible it would be no one but

Slaughter. His own part in this double-cross instigated by C would go totally unknown. Suddenly, as the spring sun broke the dawn greyness, he felt happy. The batman who had been allotted to him at GHQ could rustle up a large breakfast of looted German eggs, washed down with a stiff whisky. Then he would be in exactly the right mood to tackle the nubile teenage ATS who had been giving him the eye the day before. Abruptly, for no reason whatever, he cried to the dead cow lying in the shell-holed field to his right, its legs sticking stiffly and absurdly upright, *'Floreat Eton!'*

Three

The men were waiting for him when he surfaced at the same spot where he had left them three hours before. Eagerly they helped him aboard the first skimmer. He removed his mask and looked at their tough, weathered faces. They looked concerned. Slaughter forced a weary grin. 'All right, lads, I'm like the proverbial bad penny. I'm back.'

Staff Sergeant Williams, dark-faced and lean, his head shaven like an American, said, 'Well there's bin a lot of shit flying around, skipper. It's stopped now though.'

Slaughter looked around. It was broad daylight now and he realized that they could not stop here, just opposite the German positions on the cliffs. Still, he knew he had to brief them, especially Williams who was in charge of the second skimmer, hidden in the foliage of the bank behind them.

'All right, I've cleared a section of the boom. Big enough for us to get through. But we've got to take it easy, Williams, and you, too, Corporal Young.' He indicated the other NCO, a newcomer to the SBS, who was to steer Number One Skimmer. 'There are several loose mines just below the surface and I think they could give us a nasty kick up the arse if one of 'em went up.' He smiled.

Young didn't return his smile. His unlined face remained earnest. Slaughter knew why. He wanted to prove himself to these veterans, all of whom had seen action in the Med. 'You can depend upon me, sir,' he responded.

The others grinned. Young was a little regimental for them. Slaughter was not one for formality. Most of them called him 'skipper' anyway, ignoring his rank. Not Young, however, but then the veterans told themselves he'd learn – if he survived.

On the far bank, which was held by the Germans, a slow-moving truck, powered by a great bag of gas towed behind it on a trailer, was crawling along the heights. Slaughter guessed right away that it was some sort of mobile patrol on the lookout for any further British activity after the abortive attempt to take the railway bridge at Lauenburg. He had to make it snappy. Sooner or later the Germans would spot the two strange craft. 'OK,' he snapped. 'This is the drill in case we get spotted. Take note, especially you, Young.'

'Sir!'

'We leave the Elbe at the Trave-Kanal. Tricky, I know, dead straight in places, and narrow. No matter. On into the bay at Lubeck. Reach Travemunde and then head for Wismar Bay. If we're separated, we rendezvous at Wismar. We'll worry about our next move when we reach Wismar. With a bit of luck, we'll make it by nightfall. Rest and set out into the Baltic before dawn. Go easy on the rations for the time being. When they're finished we'll scrounge what we can.' Slaughter rapped out his orders in a swift staccato, keeping his gaze on the slow-moving truck as he did so.

His men listened attentively, absorbing the information, though Young looked as if he would have liked to have written the orders down. But that was forbidden. Slaughter had insisted on that from the start, telling his men back at Poole when they had been first alerted for this mission, 'Nothing on paper. Any written evidence that the Jerries can find, the better for them and the worse for you.' He had fixed them with a hard look in his grey eyes. 'Remember, although we'll be in uniform, the German authorities now think they have the power to execute us ever since Hitler issued his "Commando Order". To them we're spies. Most smart German commanders won't carry out that order. They know it's against the Geneva Convention. But if they've got any written evidence, the Gestapo might force them to shoot us as agents and saboteurs. Don't give the Gestapo bastards that opportunity.' Then, two weeks before, Slaughter had had a fleeting feeling that Corporal Young had been worried by his warning. Now he realized that the youngest member of the team was worried only that he might forget something and not be able to carry out the orders.

'That's it,' Slaughter concluded, pulling off his wet suit and slipping into his warm camouflaged jacket. 'Take over, Williams.'

'Yes, skipper.' Williams didn't waste time. He knew the danger they faced here in the open, with only poor camouflage to hide the outline of the two craft. He opened up. There was the soft throb of the Thorneycroft engine. A moment later Number One Skimmer was off. A couple of seconds after that, Young was steering his own vessel in the first skimmer's wake. They were on their way.

Despite the fact that there were thousands, perhaps hundreds of thousands of

German troops in the area between Berlin and Hamburg that was still unconquered by Allied troops, the countryside on the Mecklenburg side of the River Elbe was strangely deserted. Occasionally, as the two secret craft – well camouflaged now with foliage and grass sods – purred their way up the Trave-Kanal, the SBS men caught sight of German civilian convoys on the country roads, trying to escape the Russians advancing from the east towards the Baltic. But around the strategically important waterway there seemed to be no German troops at all. Even the *Volkssturm*, the enemy's home guard, which might well have guarded the locks and pumping stations of the canal, were absent. Indeed after manhandling the superlight craft cross-country when they sighted the first lock, only to find later when they were panting and sweating with the effort that it was empty (even the lockkeeper had vanished in a hurry, or so it seemed from the warm stewpot on his pot-bellied stove) they had decided it was not necessary to circumvent the locks. It was only that same afternoon, when they spotted a couple of Typhoons beating up a lock, zooming in at zero feet, cannon chattering sudden-death, that they realized the RAF dominated the skies over Mecklenburg.

That had resulted in troops steering well clear of anything that might look like a military target for the marauding British fighter-bombers.

So while the two men on duty kept watch, the rest of the SBS troopers relaxed, enjoying the thin spring sunshine, occasionally searching the flat boring Mecklenburg countryside for something of interest. Once Staff Sergeant Williams asked Slaughter's permission to halt the craft while he recced a nearby farm for eggs – 'perhaps even a chicken, sir; the lads are getting heartily sick of the compo rations. If I eat another bloody soya link, I swear I'll turn into a soya bean myself' – but the looting expedition turned out to be a failure.

'All I could find, sir,' Williams said as they set off again, 'was a few mouldy old spuds and this.' He held up a splendid-looking egg.

The others wolf-whistled like they might at the sight of a sexy blonde, and someone breathed, 'Christ, a real egg! You lucky sod, Williams.'

Sadly, Williams had shaken his head. He rapped his knuckle against the precious find. It gave a crystal-clear *ding*. 'Pot,' he said. 'A bloody pot egg. Trust old Jerry to make a perfect pot egg.'

They had laughed and begun to break out another wooden case of the boring predict- able compo ration tins.

Another dawn. The wind had died to a cold, faint breeze. Now a long swell, grey and somehow menacing, rolled from the land. The shore was still invisible, but it was there, Slaughter knew, covered still by the dawn mist. And for that Slaughter was glad. There were plenty of fishing villages and hamlets over there along the Bay of Lubeck and he didn't want his craft to be spotted.

But at the moment the only sound was the soft throb of their engines and the wild rising cries of the gulls. They dived, circled and swept the length of the two skimmers as if sounding an alarm, warning the enemy of the presence of these two strange intruders in these forbidden grey waters.

Now all the men were on duty, manning the crafts' machine guns, keeping watch, on the lookout for the first sign of danger. Savage stood next to Young at the controls, sipping a cup of muddy compo tea laced with the tot of GS rum that was given to all troops on front-line duty. After the years in the Med he felt the cold acutely and the Bay of Lubeck seemed decidedly cold. He had not realized that the Baltic could be that bloody freezing. He wouldn't be surprised if he got frostbite if the sun didn't warm the place soon. Young didn't seem to notice the cold. He was too concerned with steering a correct course, hardly daring to take his eyes off the green-glowing dials in front of him. Slaughter blew into the mug so that the steam from the compo tea blew up and warmed his red nose.

'Why did you volunteer for the mob?' he asked. 'Normally we get old hands who're sick of their old mob – marines, paras and the like.'

Still Young didn't take his gaze off the controls. 'I wanted to see action as soon as possible, sir,' he answered. 'My dad won the D.C.M. in the Great War. I thought I might do something brave in this and please him, if you know what I mean, sir,' he ended lamely and actually blushed.

Slaughter was not a sentimental or emotional man. The war had seen to that. Still, his heart went out to the young corporal, trying to prove himself to his father. He'd seen young would-be heroes like that before. Most of them were long dead now. He lowered his mug and said, 'Don't go getting any wild ideas, Corporal. You've already proved yourself by getting a corporal's stripes at your age.' Young blushed even more. 'I don't want you to do anything foolish in order to win a gong. After all, they're usually awarded posthumously—' He stopped short, nearly dropping his mug in surprise.

Edging its way out of the grey gloom of the seascape was a sharp-prowed lean craft with two quick-firers mounted just below its bridge. Slaughter didn't need to see the newcomer's crooked cross flag to know that it was German – an S-boat of the *Kriegsmarine*.

'Christ Almighty, Young, a Jerry!' he hissed.

Young reacted instinctively. He opened up the throttle. Behind them Williams at the control of Number Two Skimmer, did the same. The deck beneath Slaughter quivered abruptly. He flung a glance to the shore, now clearly visible. He calculated it was about half a mile away. 'We're going to make a run for it, Young.'

'Yessir,' Young answered and opened the throttle even more.

From the German S-boat came the faint sound of an electric klaxon shrieking the alarm. The S-boat started to turn in a great white swathe of angry water. They had been spotted and, with an urgent sensation of potential disaster, Slaughter knew the race was on. He knew they couldn't tackle the

German craft with its 20mm cannon. They had to use their speed and the fact that the secret skimmer could also hurtle across the land to escape. But they had to reach the shore first and already he could see, as he flung a look over his shoulder, the German sailors running to man the twin cannon. Even though their own maximum speed was perhaps three to five knots more than the Germans' it was going to be damned nip and tuck once the S-boat got within firing range.

Behind in Number Two Skimmer, 'Spiv' Higgins, the smart little cockney barrow boy, swung himself behind the deck Bren gun with practised ease. He opened up immediately with a cocky, 'Try this one on for size, old mate!' Instantly white tracer zipped flatly through the gloom towards the racing S-boat. A few slugs pattered off the German craft's sides, but most of the volley fell short. But that first burst only provoked S-boat's own attack.

With the traditional speed and expertise of the German gunners, a stream of tracer ripped the sea apart in a white fury to the leading skimmer's front. Skilfully, Young and Williams steered their craft through the great spouts of water that came hurtling down to drench the others on deck, waiting

123

for the S-boat to come within range so that they could engage it. Slaughter didn't give much for their chances of doing any great harm to their pursuer. At the speed they were going they would be able to keep the S-boat at a distance, too great for the machine-gunners on the skimmers to do much good. But it was the damned German gunners that worried him. He knew what they were about. They were ranging in on the skimmers.

Next moment he knew he was right. Another salvo from the Germans' twin 20mm cannon peppered the sea just behind Number Two Skimmer, and this time the salvo was much closer. Soon, if they didn't do anything about it, the enemy gunners would plant another volley right in the middle of the two fleeing craft.

'Young!' Slaughter shouted urgently. 'Try to shake those damned gunners off!'

Young, inexperienced though he was, didn't need any further instructions. Hastily he swung the craft from one side to another. The skinner responded at once. Violently the deck quivered. The prow hit the waves as if striking a solid brick wall. Slaughter felt that familiar nausea rising in his stomach as he grabbed a stanchion to prevent himself falling. Behind them, Williams, the old hand, did the same. Just in time. The next salvo struck the sea uselessly just where Number Two Skimmer had been seconds before. Williams grinned and yelled at no one in particular, 'You'll have to get up earlier, boyo, to catch Ma Williams' handsome son!'

But already the German gunners on the S-boat were adjusting their aim and on the small bridge, the Aldis lamp was flickering off and on urgently. Slaughter guessed why. Their signaller was sending a message to the land ahead. If they were not careful, the skimmers were going to be trapped between the devil and the deep blue sea, and this devil would be waiting for them on the land. What in hell's name was he going to do?

Four

The ancient wood-burning truck bumped up the rutted cliff road to the camp. It was typical of the hundreds of camps that criss-crossed Germany in 1945. It consisted of several acres of hard-packed earth (or sometimes ankle-deep mud), shaped into the form of a hexagon by the high, triple-wire fence that surrounded it. At regular intervals along the fence, which was electrified in places, there were stork-legged wooden towers, guarded by elderly reservists or mutilated young veterans of the Russian front, armed with machine guns and machine pistols. In between the inner and outer fences, fierce Alsatian dogs patrolled, attached to the safe wire by a chain. These dogs were specifically trained to go for a man's throat – or his testicles!

Inside this makeshift compound there were lines of dark wooden huts, built on piles so that the German guards, younger men, mostly SS now, could probe easily with their metal rods for contraband or attempted escapers. Between these lines, emaciated prisoners, some in civilian clothes, others in tattered uniforms, and some in the striped pyjamas of the concentration camps walked. All of them moved listlessly, as if they were in the last stages of exhaustion, which they probably were. As the gate swung open to allow the ancient truck with its occupants to enter, most of the prisoners exhibited no curiosity. Even those who did moved their heads with exquisite slowness, as if it took a great effort of will to do so.

Lofty, clutching her precious half loaf of black bread and tin of sardines – the day's ration – between her skinny arms, *was* curious, however. She knew part of the trick of surviving was to keep alert, try to outguess the enemy, reason what he was going to do next before he did it. Now she stared at their new camp, with the sea only half a mile or so away, and wondered why they, out of the thousands of pathetic wretches at their former place of imprisonment, had been selected to be sent here, to what looked like a former Stalag*, whose prisoners had been evacuated already and replaced by new

* Allied prisoner-of-war camp.

inmates, most of whom didn't look like the typical concentration-camp prisoner.

Suddenly she felt fear pricking her skin. Instinctively she knew that there was something wrong about this new camp. Was it one of those *Sonderlagers*, those special camps reserved for special prisoners? Lofty didn't have time to find out. Fat Otto, half-drunk as usual, sitting at the back with the SOE prisoners, said, rising unsteadily to his feet as the truck finally stopped, 'Ladies, I am now leaving you. For ever.' He sniffed, as though overcome with emotion, and Lofty's neighbour, Rosie, handed him back his bayoneted rifle. 'I am not happy at saying goodbye,' he quavered. 'I have liked you.'

Rosie, the bitter realist, said, 'Och aye, ye'll be off to the Russian front nae doubt.'

Fat Otto shook his head ponderously. 'No, not that. It is you ladies, I miss.' He shook his head until his fat jowls wobbled. 'Yes, you ladies. When I come back to the Savoy I ask about you.' Again he shook his head and Rosie couldn't stop herself from interjecting. '*If* you come back.'

Fat Otto didn't seem to hear. Sadly he wandered off, trailing his rifle behind him. 'Poor old sod,' Nellie Dean said. But Rosie shook her head and commented, 'It's poor, sentimental old German sods like that stuff kids into the ovens.'

For what seemed a long time the women sat in their truck, listening to the roar of the sea in the distance and the gruff orders of the guards, who again were SS, but this time younger and more military. Lofty could see that although most of them had obviously been downgraded due to wounds received in battle, they were still alert and on their toes. They couldn't expect to receive much mercy from these SS men if they attempted to escape; and escape they must, for Lofty had a sneaking suspicion that the new camp was intended for those the Nazis wanted to get rid of as soon as possible. But for the moment she wasn't going to alarm the others with her suspicions. The poor dears had problems enough as it was...

They knew the German was the inter-rogator, although he didn't say what his function was straight away. They had seen the type often enough before when they had been captured back in France the previous autumn. They all seemed to run to the same type: chummy, with the look of an ex-schoolteacher about them. And *Hauptmann* Fischer, who affected a warm smile and a friendly manner, though his eyes behind his pince-nez remained cold, appeared to be no different.

Immediately the women had been lined up in front of him, he gushed, 'Well, ladies, I have myself once lived in England – in your beautiful Oxford. We shall be friends, yes?' He beamed at the emaciated women prisoners, as if they might well rush forward after such an announcement and demand to shake his hand.

'Romantic Oxford ... Dreamy spires and all that, sir,' Rosie said cynically.

'Yes ... yes.' He took the bait. 'I have indeed spent the best days of my youth there.'

Lofty flashed Rosie a warning look. She knew the *Hauptmann* Fischers of this world. He was giving them the old sweet/sour routine, and Fischers could turn sour as speedily as they could sweet if things didn't go the way they wanted. The less one said to such types the better.

But Rosie, as aggressive as always and knowing that Fischer was admiring those wonderful breasts of hers, was not going to be put down. 'I suppose, sir, that you are a friend of England and regret this terrible war betwen our two countries?'

Fischer rose to the bait like a trout rising to an attractive fly, 'Yes, young lady, you are being very right. Our two peoples should be fighting those sub-humans, the Russians, and not each other. Now I am not wanting to make life hard for you, ladies, especially as you are English and not that eastern pack of sub-humans out there.' He indicated the subdued, ragged prisoners outside, who were now beginning to line up for the usual midday soup from the great steaming cauldrons, the surface of the witch's brew crawling with weevils and other insects. 'You obey orders and I am your friend.' He licked his thick, sensual lips as he eyed Rosie's bosom again. 'Disobey and I am unpleasant.'

'You mean you want to fuck us—'

'*Rosie!*' Lofty cried, but Rosie wasn't listening.

'Before you bash our brains out, man,' she continued.

Hauptmann Fischer looked bewildered. '*Fuck?* What is this fuck?' he queried. 'I am not understanding.'

Before a worried Lofty could stop her, Rosie had made her meaning quite clear. She made a circle with the thumb and forefinger of one hand and thrust the middle finger of her other hand in and out of the circle several times. 'Get the idea, *Herr Hauptmann?*'

131

Hauptmann Fischer spluttered with rage. 'I am not doing such things!' he cried. 'You are my enemy. It is forbidden.'

Lofty shook her head at the thick-headedness of the Germans. They might send thousands of women to their deaths in the most cruel manner, but their code of discipline – or whatever they called it – wouldn't allow them to even think of sexually abusing them, although their female prisoners would be totally powerless to stop them.

Fischer calmed himself a little. 'You will now be searched,' he announced, adopting his 'sour' manner. 'Thereafter you will return to your truck and be taken for delousing. We Germans look after our prisoners.'

The women didn't respond. They had become subdued at the thought of the search and the delousing process; they were very humiliating.

Hauptmann Fischer took one last look at them before dismissing them to the waiting sergeant, a middle-aged *Wehrmacht* soldier with a gross face, hanging beer belly and an unpleasant grin. Fischer clicked his heels together and gave them a slight salute, saying, 'I am now reporting that you are here to SS Headquarters in Berlin.'

At that moment they weren't one bit

interested where the ex-schoolmaster might report to. Only later would they learn that Fischer's report to Berlin had started the long process of their liberation. Fischer would – indirectly – be responsible for saving their lives.

The fat sergeant threw Fischer a salute and then, spitting out the unlit stub of a cheap cigar from his slack lips, he barked, '*Los ... wird's bald? ... Runter mit den Hosen.*' He pointed to Lofty. 'You ... you first.'

Lofty felt herself go weak as the fat sergeant pulled on his fingerstall, an evil grin on his face. How could she lift up her striped skirt, pull down her knickers and expose her shaven pubes to this gross creature? The shame of it, out here in the open. But then she remembered the razor blade hidden in the instep of her wooden clog: that was to be her last resort, the final way out. Blinded with tears, gritting her teeth, she did as he required of her. A moment later he was probing her vagina, grunting like the pig he was.

It was an hour later, while they were finding their way around their new home – a hut adorned with the photographs, pornographic drawings, regimental badges of those soldier prisoners-of-war who had been incarcerated there – that it happened.

133

Some of them had busied themselves trying to rid themselves of the delousing powder that had been pumped down their backs, breasts and between their legs. Others had, perhaps foolishly scrounged for any food that the soldiers might have left behind, while others had tried to assemble complete bunks, taking planks from one bunk to fill the gaps in the one they had selected for themselves.

They didn't talk much. They were still overwhelmed by the physical examination and the delousing process that had taken place in front of half a dozen German soldiers who admired their nakedness, though, as Nellie Dean commented, 'I don't know what they saw in us. We're all just skin and bones.'

'Except me,' Rosie had interrupted, as always full of that tough Scottish fighting spirit.

They heard the sharp warning hiss of breath outside quite clearly, despite the roar of the sea. Lofty turned swiftly. 'What was that?'

By way of answer there was the sound of breaking glass. Next moment a rock came flying through one of the windows and landed in the middle of the floor at Lisa's feet.

For what seemed a long time the women stared, mesmerized, at the rock, as if they feared it might be some sort of German trick, a disguised bomb or grenade. But when nothing happened, Rosie said, 'I'll get it, girls.'

She stooped and picked up the rock and for the first time they saw there was a scrap of dirty packing paper attached to it. Wordlessly, Rosie held it up to the light from outside and read what had been scrawled on it with soot from one of the stovepipes. *'Get out,'* she read. *'Danger now ... A friend.'*

They stared at each other in awed silence until Nellie Dean turned to Lofty, their unspoken leader, and asked, 'Well, what do *you* think, Lofty? After all, it's in English.'

The tall SOE agent hesitated only a second. In a toneless voice, without emotion, she answered, 'I think we'd better take it seriously...'

Five

'It's a damned nuisance,' C said slowly, considering the impact of every word he uttered before he said it, while Fleming waited in the dark room, sitting in front of the desk that had once belonged to Admiral Nelson.

As he had expected, from what he had learned from his colleagues in Naval Intelligence, he had passed through the warren of passages that was the Special Intelligence Service's HQ at 21 Queen Anne's Gate.

C's office was large but by some trick of the lighting everything seemed to be in silhouette. A line of telephones on extensions stood to the left of Nelson's oak desk while to the right there was a smaller desk covered with models of aeroplanes and bottles that reminded Fleming of the chemy labs at Eton. Did C carry out scientific experiments like some of his predecessors had done? Whatever went on here, everything, Fleming told himself, added to the place's overpowering atmosphere of strangeness and mystery. While he waited for C to explain why he had been summoned here at this ungodly hour, he tried to etch the place on his mind's eye. It would be useful in his writing one day, he knew that.

'A damned nuisance,' C repeated, 'something I could have done without at this stage of the game.'

Fleming would dearly have loved to ask what was a nuisance and what the game was, but he held his peace. He knew that men like C, self-important men who had connections at court, the old boys' network, clubland and the city, didn't like to be interrupted by people like Fleming, even if they were fellow old-Etonians.

'You know about Bletchley ... the Ultra operation?' C asked, abruptly staring him in the face for the first time since the green light outside C's office had flickered off and on, indicating that Fleming could enter.

'Yessir.'

'Well, you know what we do there?'

'Yessir, you read Germany's most secret coded messages.'

C allowed himself a wintry smile. 'Yes, even before the people they are addressed to have them deciphered, eh?' His smile vanished as soon as it had appeared. Suddenly his grey face was pinched and taut. The wrinkles of worry seemed to increase around his cold grey eyes. 'Early this morning, Fleming, I and the PM received this from Bletchley. You shouldn't read it, I know, but I'm giving you permission to do so. It's an Ultra.'

Fleming was overcome by a strange feeling, almost the same as when a new woman opened her legs and one knew that one was going to have her, be initiated into the mystery of a new body. With a right hand that trembled slightly he accepted the flimsy paper and read it. He could see immediately it was top-level stuff, addressed to SS HQ at Hohenlychen just outside Berlin, though the signal itself wasn't so important. It stated simply: SOE prisoners arrived at former Stalag VIIIa. Request instructions for further 'treatment'.

C saw Fleming's look. He said, 'It's the word "treatment". It means get rid of these SOE women. Now our problem is that the PM knows what the German buggers intend to do with them, and as usual he wants action. So, Fleming, we can't just let it go ahead as ... er ... planned. We must be seen to be doing more.'

'I see, sir,' Fleming said, though he really didn't understand.

'Now, we know where these women have

been taken. It is a former Anglo-American POW camp, which was evacuated by the Germans in February when the Reds started their attacks in East Prussia and Pomerania in earnest. The poor devils are probably still marching westwards across Germany at this moment. No matter. Come over here and look at the map.'

Obediently, Fleming followed the old man – who seemed to creak when he walked – to the big wall map of Central Europe. He pointed a skeletal finger at the map. 'Now here, at the far end of the Baltic, the Russian Army is breaking out of East Prussia into Pomerania. Here and there they're being held up at cities such as Konigsberg and Danzig. But not for long. In essence, the Germans are in full retreat westwards, knowing that once the Red Army surrounds Berlin, they'll be cut off in the far north.'

Fleming nodded his understanding and C went on, tracing the coastline with his fore-finger. 'The Hun is using all these little ports – Peenemunde, Swinemunde, etcetera, to embark as many fugitives, refugees and Wehrmacht units as possible, in order to get them to the west before the Russians close in. Naturally the Baltic is alive with Soviet submarines, but that's the risk the Hun is prepared to take, and anyway,

Admiral Doenitz –' Fleming knew he referred to the fanatical Nazi admiral who was now in charge of the western part of Germany not yet conquered by the British – 'has got his whole fleet in the Baltic protecting the Hun convoys.

'Now that's the general military naval position, Fleming. So where is this Stalag VIIIa?' He answered his own question. Pointing his bony finger forward, he indicated a point just above the Baltic port of Swinemunde. 'It's there. I have asked MI9,' he meant the intelligence department concerned with British POWs in Germany, 'what they know about it. They say it is a small camp some half a mile from the port, according to the secret messages our POWs smuggled out of the place while they were. They regarded it as an easy place to get out of, though the catch was what were they going to do once they had got through the wire.' He paused and looked keenly at the younger officer, as if he half expected Fleming to be able to read his somewhat devious thoughts.

But Fleming wasn't able to do so. With a little sigh, C continued, 'So let us say we directed Captain Slaughter and his skimmer crews to this camp – there are numerous waterways leading from the coast in the general direction of Stalag VIIIa – and they succeeded in rescuing these damned women, the PM would certainly be pleased. As far as he was concerned, we would have carried out the rescue mission as ordered. But if thereafter they faced the same problems as did our POWs there when they escaped—'

'The German Navy in the Baltic?'

For a moment even C's grey face seemed to light up. 'Exactly, Fleming.'

'And if disaster then overtook them—'

'We couldn't be faulted for the failure of Slaughter and his men,' C said, beating him to it. 'The matter would be out of our control. The PM would just have to accept the fact that we had done our best and we had failed. We'd be off the hook, Fleming.'

As cynical and hard-bitten as he was, Fleming was shaken by the cold-blooded deviousness of the spymaster. Etonians, as he knew well, were supposed to be reserved in a superior kind of way, never displaying their true feelings; it wasn't the done thing. But Fleming had never met anyone from the old school who had been as patently and unfeelingly cold-blooded as the old grey man now hunched in the chair opposite him.

For a moment or two there was silence in

that hidden room. In the end, Fleming felt obliged to say something to break that brooding silence. He said, 'But can we direct Slaughter and his skimmers to this Stalag VIIIa, sir?'

'Yes. He has with him one of our new long-range radio sets, which he has been instructed to use only in an emergency. The Huns' direction-finding chaps are top quality. They'd soon home in on him if he were to use the wireless for long or too frequently. Now, Fleming, we're going to contact Slaughter, wherever he is, and inform him about Stalag VIIIa. Unfortunately, the transmission will perforce have to be somewhat lengthy.' C paused and gave Fleming a significant look before continuing. 'But we'll have to take that risk to show the PM we have been doing our job properly.'

Suddenly it dawned on Fleming why C had just looked at him so significantly. *He wanted the German direction-finding team to track Slaughter down!*

They had been damned lucky, Slaughter would have been the first to admit, though the big tough SBS officer believed that you made your own luck. Just as the German S-boat had been in the final stage of ranging on the fleeing skimmers, they had hit the shore and the new mechanism that allowed the two craft to skim just above the ground had kicked in. In addition, the shoreline had been typical for that area: a great stretch of white sand with the dunes as the only dangerous obstacle.

Furiously, as the S-boat had swung round in a graceful curl of white water, its skipper had ordered his crews to pepper the beach. To no avail. The two skimmers had cleared the first of the dunes like a thoroughbred steeplechaser sweeping easily over a high fence and vanished over the other side.

For a while they had continued their crazy pace up the beach, taking hair-raising risks of hitting an obstacle. For Slaughter knew the frustrated skipper of the S-boat would attempt to raise some ground troops on-shore to stop them. But again, the SBS men seemed to have struck lucky. The area seemed deserted. Here and there they had spotted a fisherman's cottage, the usual one-storey, whitewashed structure, but their straw roofs had vanished to reveal charred, blackened beams as if they had been aflame at some point.

In the end they had found a stretch of water leading down to the sea, fortunately protected and hidden on both sides by white dunes, flecked by clumps of razor-sharp high grass. Here Slaughter had ordered them to cut engines, followed by the traditional issue of rum from the great gallon flagon, jealously guarded by Staff Sergeant Williams, who, the other crew members said, was indulging himself in the fiery rum and watering it down in due course.

Slaughter, accompanied by Corporal Young, who naturally didn't drink (he'd swapped his rum ration for a portion of nuts and raisins with Spiv), checked out the area where they had hidden the skimmers. The air was full of the heady, spicy smell of wild herbs and pine resin from the pine forest in the distance. It was as good a hiding place as any, Slaughter thought, though he was still puzzled by the empty, burned-out cottages and the absence of farmers, though he had to admit the land didn't seem capable of growing much more than potatoes and beets. Anyway, he told himself, it didn't matter. They wouldn't be able to stay here very long. Surely the S-boat skipper would have alerted the authorities by now to send out search parties to look for the intruders. Even in what he took to be the confusion of the great Baltic evacuation from east to west, there'd be enough German troops for that. Besides, there would always be the local *Volkssturm* if the *Wehrmacht* regulars were in short supply.

The question that now worried him most was where were they to head for next? Their briefing by that upper-class bugger Fleming, with his cigarette holder and his other foppish mannerisms, had been vague. Would it be time to open up his long-range radio, which he knew had to be used only in an emergency, and ask for any further information about the imprisoned women that might have come in in the meantime? He frowned and stopped so abruptly that Young, his tommy gun cradled across his arm, almost bumped into him. The latter murmured an apology and Slaughter, who had taken to the green volunteer, said, 'My fault, Corporal. Preoccupied with my own thoughts, I suppose.'

'Problems, sir?'

'Not really,' Slaughter answered with a dry little laugh. 'Only the usual one of how to survive till tomorrow morning.'

Young's face still remained serious; he wasn't given to much humour. 'Are we in trouble, sir?'

Before Slaughter could answer, there was a screech of aeroplane engines going all-out. A plane appeared from nowhere. It raced

145

across the barren coastal landscape at an incredible speed. Almost as soon as it arrived it seemed to disappear, but not before the cannon shells erupted all around the two lone Englishmen in a lethal fury.

'Christ, sir!' Young cried as the plane turned in a tight curve, trailing dark smoke behind it. 'The bugger's got no engine. What is it?'

Slaughter had no time to enlighten him. Young had seen his first jet, and that jet was coming in for the attack once more, and they might not be so lucky this time. Now he knew why the cottages were missing their straw roofs. This was a firing range for the new German secret weapons, and that jet pilot's aim might not be so uncertain on his second run.

'Run!' he cried. 'Run like hell ... Back to the boats! *Run!*'

Six

'I once knew a Judy,' Spiv was saying, 'who had four nipples and two pairs of tits.' The little Cockney SBS trooper formed a large arc in the air. 'Christ Almighty, she had the kind of tits yer could have put yer head between and never heard another sound for a fortnight.'

Corporal Young frowned. He knew the older men always talked like that when they were off watch, but he didn't like it. Women were supposed to be respected. Besides, he had never gone further with a girl than reaching up to the top of her stockings in an air-raid shelter during a raid on Pompey back in '44. He'd nearly died with the excitement of it all. He'd been forced to keep his hands off his groin every time he thought of the feel of his rough palm against the smoothness of her silk stockings, fingertips striving for the soft, hot flesh beyond. He tried to concentrate on the threepenny Woolworths German dictionary he had brought with him on this op in an attempt to improve himself. *'Der Tisch,'* he repeated to himself. *'Den Tisch ... Des Tisches.'*

Spiv, meanwhile, was saying, 'Mind yer, lads, it was a funny feeling playing with four tits. I mean, a bloke really needed more fingers ... I mean, all them nipples! Yer didn't know which one to play with first.'

'What about the other bit?' another of the SBS troopers queried.

Slaughter shook his head, a slight smile on his face. As long as the men were complaining about the food and getting excited by talking about sex, everything was well with his skimmer crews. He need not fear about their morale. He dismissed Spiv and his preoccupation with 'number one', as they called sex, and returned to his map of the Baltic.

They had escaped from their hiding place without being bothered by the new-fangled German jets again, but he felt these tremendously fast planes, which were flying from some secret experimental station in the area, might well be equipped with cameras. If they were, the one they'd seen might well have spotted them and reported the sighting to local headquarters. If it had, German Intelligence would have put two and two together and reasoned that the

Tommies had survived the S-boat attack. The German Navy would be looking for the skimmers once more. If that were the case, it seemed sensible to Captain Slaughter to keep close to the land, where in an emergency he could use the skimmers' ability to skim across level surfaces. The disadvantage was that by closely following the coastline, he would of necessity lengthen the time it would take to carry out any rescue, and Slaughter didn't need a crystal ball to know that the inland sea was a watery trap. There was only one way into it and one way out of it by boat – the narrows of the Skagerak between Sweden and Denmark – and for the time being the German Navy controlled that particular dangerous exit.

Slaughter frowned and stared hard at the map of the coastline to the east. There were several waterways leading from the Baltic and slightly inland, especially in the Peenemunde area. Indeed there was what looked like a large internal lake after Peenemunde, which ran for miles until it exited at Anklam. He guessed that larger German naval ships wouldn't be able to use its more shallow waters. Besides, if the German Navy was preoccupied with escorting vessels bringing soldiers, refugees and the like from the east, the Jerries would be concentrating all available naval craft in the Baltic itself. Why waste ships on an inland sea?

He sniffed and concentrated on the problem, while Spiv continued with his story. But the others were getting bored. They had already broken into one of the compo ration boxes and were selecting the best of the tins it contained for their midday meal.

'Amoured pig?' Someone suggested, referring to the everpresent Spam.

'Not on yer frigging nelly,' another of the SBS troopers objected. 'I've eaten so much of that bloody stuff I'm beginning to honk like a frigging porker.'

'Meat and veg, then...' but the words died on the man's lips as Staff Sergeant Williams yelled urgently, 'Sir, we've got someone on the blower!'

The chat ceased immediately. They all knew that this was the first time they had been contacted by long-distance radio. This had to be important, especially as any radio message might well give their position away to the German naval direction service at Murwik Station in Schleswig-Holstein at the other side of the Baltic.

Hastily Slaughter dropped his map and, pushing Young and his dictionary to one side, he grabbed the earphone set from Williams.

'Sunray,' he called, hoping that if any German *was* picking up the message, he'd think that by some freak of the airwaves he had located some low-level infantry G.O. 'Sunray here ... over.'

'Sunray Two ... Sunray One here.' The voice was distorted, but Slaughter guessed it belonged to one of Fleming's naval signallers, calling from the top of the Admiralty, where the brass had their wireless station. He reasoned the man was used to naval signals where there wasn't the urgency of flashing a signal over the airwaves so that any listening enemy could not get a fix on it. This unknown naval signaller was taking his time – too much time. It would take only a few moments more and Murwik would be attempting to locate the recipient of the signal.

'Hello Sunray Two,' he called urgently, throwing radio procedure to the winds. 'Get cracking ... chop chop ... over.'

Two minutes later he had the signal and, even before he had fully digested it, he was calling to Williams and Young. 'All right, lads, let's get moving ... *Move it!*'

And move it they did. They realized the urgency of the situation. They were on their way again, with each man wrapped up in a cocoon of his own thoughts and apprehensions. For even the greenhorn like Corporal Young realized that the deeper they entered the Baltic, the less chance they had of getting out of the inland sea alive.

.They had left Peenemunde behind them now, crawling at a snail's pace through the still water of the inland sea in order not to create a telltale wake. Not that Peenemunde should have worried them. It was once again a fiery blaze on the horizon as the Red air force bombed it, just as the RAF had been doing periodically since mid-1944. Neither the British nor their Russian allies wanted to let the great experimental station where the Germans had produced their 'revenge weapons' – the V-1 and the even more deadly V-2 – to start up again. After all, only days before, a German V-2 missile had landed on London.

In silence the off-duty watches surveyed the burning ruin, a stark black jumble of bombed installations outlined against the cherry-red flames of the new inferno. Not one of them, even Young, felt one ounce of pity for the hundreds of humans who might well be perishing there at this very moment. As Spiv expressed it, remembering his grey-haired mother who had been killed in one of the first V-1 attacks on the British capital the previous summer, 'A nice clean bomb is too good for those bastards yonder. I hope they roast in hell – *slowly*.'

But Slaughter had no time to dwell on such thoughts of revenge. He was concerned with getting through the inner lake before dawn. Admittedly, he wasn't worried about naval craft, but he was worried about troops on land. If this was one of the major evacuation areas for the *Wehrmacht*, frantically attempting to transport as many troops as possible to the west before the Red army arrived on the scene, there ought to be enemy soldiers everywhere, especially on the narrow coastal strip from Peenemunde to Ahlbeck.

Slaughter reasoned it would be safer for the skimmers if they kept close to the far shore in the general area of the Red army's advance. Any German troops to be found there would be too occupied with the Russians to be concerned with what was going on behind them on the inner lake. Unconsciously he crossed his fingers behind his back and hoped he was right.

That night passed quietly enough on the inner sea. All around, it seemed to the SBS on watch that there was plenty going on. To port, where the Russians were advancing, the horizon remained a flickering pink, indicating that an attack was in process, and when the wind was in the right direction they could hear the muted rumble of heavy artillery. To starboard there were lights out to sea and every now and again searchlights flicked and flashed upwards, as if searching for planes, and again there was the rumble of artillery as a brief fire-fight, perhaps between the German *Kriegsmarine* and Russian submarines or torpedo boats, took place.

At three that morning, Slaughter ordered his men to take the skimmers into a suitable cove to eat and be briefed, for he believed that his SBS troopers should know why and for what they were risking their lives. Briskly, as they ate the last of their bread with great wedges of dry cheese or bully beef, washed down with steaming hot cocoa laced with rum, he filled them in. He told them of the possible fate of the SOE women, if they weren't rescued soon, and how, according to the signal from Naval Intelligence, they were imprisoned in a former POW camp, not more than twenty miles from where they found themselves at that moment.

As Slaughter had half anticipated, these tough veterans, some of whom had wives and children of their own, were sympathetic, not in the least fazed by the dangers inherent in the rescue.

'Poor tarts,' they murmured. 'They deserve the best we can do for them ... Sodding Jerries, shooting women like that.'

Then he went into the details of his makeshift plan, which he had been trying to work out ever since they had entered the inner sea. 'My guess is, chaps, that we won't have much time to lark about. The Jerries are in full retreat. If things don't work and the Russians get too close, they'll panic and probably shoot the SOE women out of hand. They're going to shoot them or get rid of them in the end anyway, so they won't hang about waiting for orders from above to do so. They'll just do it and do a bunk while they're still safe.'

'So, sir, it's gonna be in like Flynn?' Williams suggested.

Normally there would have been a mild laugh at the reference to Errol Flynn and his alleged manner with women. But not this night. The situation, the men knew, was too grave.

'Yes, to a certain extent,' Slaughter agreed. 'But we've got to have time to recce the Stalag. I mean, we don't want to walk straight into a trap.'

There was a murmur of agreement and Young said hesitantly, blushing in the darkness, 'I'll volunteer to go, sir ... I speak some German now.'

Spiv laughed drily and added, 'Yes, don't forget to take yer dictionary with yer, Corp.'

'Quiet,' Slaughter snapped. 'Now, let's get moving again.'

Five minutes later they were on their way again, with Spiv taking obvious pleasure in describing to an off-duty Young what to do in a medical emergency. 'If yer mucker gets hit in the mug, Corp, he'll have a mouthful o' bits of bones and gristle. What you do, Corp, so that the poor shit doesn't choke to death, is to dig yer fingers down his windpipe and pull out the muck. If that don't work, take your knife and slit his throat right smartish – just beneath the Adam's apple – then slip in a tube and you'll have yer mucker breathing like a ruddy baby in no time...'

Listening, Slaughter was half-tempted to tell the little cockney to shut up and stop taking the mickey out of the green NCO, but then he thought better of it. The advice was good and Young would have to get used to the realities of combat. Military action wasn't all clean gunshot wounds through unimportant parts of the body and medals for bravery. It was a savage, bloody affair, where men died violently and in agony.

There was nothing noble about combat.

Then he dismissed the two of them and, making himself more comfortable on the hard wooden deck, he closed his eyes, telling himself that he needed all the rest he could get. On the morrow there'd be no time for kip. In time he fell asleep, making no noise as he did so as he had trained himself to do long before. Indeed, anyone viewing him lying there, with his head on a coiled pile of rope, might well have thought he was dead. Beyond where the Russians were, the noise of the guns grew louder and over the lines of the hard-pressed German defenders the signal flares asking for help came at an ever more rapid pace. The Red Army was attacking in force. It wouldn't be long now before they broke through to the inner sea and then to the Baltic coast beyond.

Slaughter slept on.

THREE

Comrade Stalin Takes a Hand

One

In the officers' brothel, the Leningrad whores sent to the front to service the Red Navy's senior officers prepared for the night's business quite openly. A couple, naked save for sheer black silk stockings, were washing themselves over buckets of steaming-hot water brought in by the German maids, scrubbing at their trimmed crotches energetically. Others, already washed, were preparing primitive contraceptives: sponges soaked in vinegar which they would insert in their vaginas when the time came. No one, even these hard-boiled Leningrad whores, who had been through the 900-day siege, wanted to give a high-ranking naval officer VD. The NKVD would ship them off to the gulag without a second thought. A few were already dressed for the night's business in black and red silk knickers, their nipples painted as bright a red as their lips.

All was hectic, noisy activity in the

requisitioned German hotel punctuated by quick puffs at the long Russian cigarettes that balanced on the ashtrays everywhere, hefty slugs of vodka and the jingle of the gypsy orchestra tuning up for the officers' entertainment.

Lieutenant Bogodan of the Soviet Red Fleet sniffed. He had been in brothels enough in his time – who else but whores would keep company with submariners, who spent most of their short, violent lives at sea before the inevitable happened? But he didn't like this high-class place with its excessive consumption and whores who would not even look at a humble lieutenant even though he commanded his own submarine and bore the medal of 'Hero of the Soviet Union' on his broad chest. Unconsciously he groped for the little bag in his tunic pocket. It was something he always did when he was upset. The bag contained a few grains of his native earth. As superstitious as all submariners were, he felt he would never rest if he weren't buried in his native earth, even just a few grains of it.

And now he was upset, for he couldn't understand why he had been invited to this high-class senior officers' brothel. Why should he meet some high-ranking official here? Such people usually attempted to conceal their way of life from humble folk like lieutenants in the submarine service. It was very strange.

'Comrade Lieutenant?' He turned, startled.

It was the whore-mother, as they called the women who ran such brothels. She was fat and old. Her hair was dyed pitch-black with henna, though the roots were still grey. Her body was strapped in by a tight pair of stays which showed through the black silk gown she wore in the fashion of the old bourgeoisie. Her nails were very long and were painted a bright scarlet; they looked as if they might well have been dipped in blood. Perhaps they had been.

'Yes, comrade,' he answered dutifully.

'He will see you now. He asked that you should be discreet. Follow me.'

Puzzled, he did so while the gypsy orchestra struck up one of those moody but wild tunes that customers in such places liked. The whore-mothers, too. It made the men sexually excited and they spent more money. In a bored manner the Leningrad whores started to move into their allotted places for the start of the night's orgy. As they passed the raddled old whore-mother, they curtsied in the pre-revolution fashion. Bogodan, the son of peasants, told himself the whore-mother had probably once carried out the same job as for men with more sophisticated tastes than her present-day clients.

He followed her down a corridor that smelled of the cigars, Munich beer, sauerkraut and sausage of its former owners, now lying stiff and dead in the backyard, shot the day before by the Red Army. She stopped before a door at the end of the corridor. Yellow light crept from beneath it, but there was no sound save for a kind of sad keening. She adjusted her tight dress, screwing the stays around and popping back her wrinkled left breast that had sprung out of her bodice with the movement. 'Discretion,' she murmured and tapped on the door.

There was no answer, but the keening stopped. She knocked again, louder this time. A gruff voice in a Moscow accent ordered, 'Come.'

Carefully the whore-mother opened the door, as though she expected the worst, the young submarine commander thought, and he was right. A girl, a German girl with blonde plaits, lay sobbing on a bed, her white knickers pulled down to reveal child's buttocks. Opposite her on the big chair, a fat officer with an evil, pock-marked face, was licking his lips, as if he had just enjoyed a good meal, fastening up his flies and looking very pleased with himself.

Bogodan knew exactly what the fat officer in the general's uniform – which had the green tabs of the feared secret police, the NKVD, on his collar – had done. He'd got the whore-mother to procure him one of the German girls who had been foolish enough to remain in the city when the Red Army had attacked and bring her to the security of the officers' brothel. The Leningrad whores were obviously too raddled and worn for his sophisticated Moscow tastes.

The NKVD general reached for an open bottle on the night table and took a drink of vodka straight from it. 'Comrade Lieutenant Bogodan?' Bogodan sprang to attention and rasped, *'Da.'*

The general took his time. He sized up the young officer, starting at his feet and raising his gaze to his face, as though assessing some damn cow in his native *Kolhoz*. Then he nodded, approving of what he saw and, turning to the whore mother, ordered, 'Get her out of here by the back. Give her some tins of meat or something and tell her to keep her mouth shut if she knows what's good for her.'

'Da, tovarich,' the old woman croaked. She put her hand, covered with liver spots, on

165

the girl's naked shoulder and said, in German – or it might have been Yiddish, for all Bogodan knew, '*Hore auf mit dem Weinen, Schiksa ... Davoi ... Los!*'

Still sobbing, the girl turned, her tiny pink-tipped breasts uncovered so that Bogodan could see the bites the general had made on them. He frowned and, although she was one of the hated Fritz, he felt that this shouldn't have happened to her; she was just a child. Automatically she pulled up her stained knickers over her bloody loins and let the old crone of a whore-mother lead her out.

The general saw the look on Bogodan's face and said, 'You might have the right name*, but you don't need to play the role. She's just a Fritz. By the time our brave boys have had her, she'll like it. Better than a piece of German salami up her any day.' He laughed coarsely. 'Now then, let's get down to business, Lieutenant.'

'Comrade?' Bogodan forced himself to say. The man made him feel sick. But at the same time, he felt a sensation of fear. 'Hero of the Soviet Union' he might be, but such things meant nothing to these Moscow generals. They'd send him to Siberia at the

* Bogdan means 'gift of god'.

drop of a hat if they felt like it. No one was safe from the clique around Stalin and Beria, the head of the Secret Police.

'You have an excellent record in the Black Sea, Bogodan,' the general said. 'We have discussed it at headquarters and have decided you are the officer we need for this mission. Indeed, I can tell you Comrade Stalin himself has looked at your record and has given his approval. Now what do you say to that, eh? What an honour.'

Mystified and bewildered, all Bogodan could stutter was, 'Yes, a great honour, Comrade General.'

Outside, in the big room with the whores and their high-ranking clients, the gypsy orchestra balalaika players were beginning to strum 'Black Eyes'. They always did on such occasions, to get their listeners ready for the orgy to come. First there'd be the sentimental stuff and then, when the vodka was starting to have its effect, they'd begin singing *'Katinka'* and some drunk would attempt a Cossack dance and promptly fall flat on his fat face. It was the kind of Russia that Bogodan hated, the kind of drunken self-indulgence that had no place in the new Russia that looked forward to a new technical age bringing happiness and prosperity to all, not just the *nomenclatura* of the Party bosses. That was what he and the other young submarine skippers were fighting for, not to preserve the old and discredited.

'What is it then that we desire of you, Comrade Lieutenant?' the NKVD general asked. Naturally, he answered his own question. 'This. You are to fly back to Leningrad this very night. We have a special plane ready for you. Your boat has already been alerted and is ready to sail within the hour.'

Bogodan opened his mouth to ask something, but decided against it. These Party bosses didn't like to be interrupted by questions from their subordinates. So he remained silent, his brain racing electrically as he wondered why he, a simple submarine skipper, was receiving such special treatment.

The NKVD general soon enlightened him. 'You remember the German ship, the *Wilhelm Gustloff*, back in January, Comrade Lieutenant?'

'Yes, Comrade General,' he answered promptly. He certainly did. The matter had been hushed up at the time, but everyone in the Red Fleet's submarine surface knew something of that terrible story. The *Wilhelm Gustloff*, named after a Swiss Nazi, had been carrying well over ten thousand passengers when she had sailed from Danzig on

January 30th. There were about one thousand officer cadets on board, but the rest of the passengers had been civilians, refugees from the Red Army trying to escape to the west. Most of them had never made it. Off the coast of Pomerania, the *Wilhelm Gustloff*, accompanied by one lone minesweeper, had been attacked by a Russian submarine. The *Gustloff* hadn't had a chance. She'd gone down, taking most of her passengers with her. In the end only six hundred had survived the freezing waters of the Baltic. As the NKVD general now reminded Bogodan, 'It was the greatest ship tragedy in history, Comrade. Five times more people drowned on the *Gustloff* than did on the *Titanic*.'

Bogodan nodded numbly, wondering again what all this had to do with him. The NKVD general enlightened him. 'Comrade Stalin wants a spectacular sinking in the Baltic,' he said. 'Something with more casualties than the *Gustloff*. Why, Comrade Lieutenant? I shall tell you. Churchill and his soldiers are trying to seal off the Baltic before we reach the exit and the North Sea. The English plutocrats are running scared.' He grinned in his lopsided sly manner. 'And so they should be. Who knows if the Red Army will stop its march westwards once we have conquered Berlin. No matter.' He dismissed the question with a wave of his big hairy paw. 'But the Fritzes are currently the problem. They are holding up our advance along the Baltic coast. The time has come to show the Fritzes that their attempts to evacuate their citizens and soldiers from east to west are futile. Convince them of that and their *Kriegsmarine* will give up and go home, leaving the Baltic to the Red Fleet and Army. After all, it was the German Imperial Fleet mutineering at their ports such as Kiel at the end of the Great War which brought about the end of the imperial monarchy and forced Germany to sue for peace...'

Although Bogodan had come to detest the NKVD general, he appreciated his reasoning. By making the Germans see that their efforts in the Baltic were pointless, the disgruntled Fritzes might well give up and leave the Red Army to hop from one German port to another, westwards, supported by the Red Fleet, and beat the English to the exit from the Baltic.

Outside, the sound of the music was getting louder and more hectic. The general pulled his tunic straighter. Obviously he wanted to be where the fun was. Perhaps he had another of these young German girls waiting for him to rape and sodomize. Bogodan wouldn't put anything past that lecherous old crone, the whore-mother.

'We have picked a vessel for you to sink, Comrade. Our spies tell us she is ready to sail at any time within the next seventy-two hours. By then you can be in position in the Baltic, yes?'

'Yes,' Bogodan agreed and waited.

The general didn't make him wait long. 'She is the *Vaterland*, a thirty-thousand tonner. She will be carrying some fifteen thousand people onboard.' For some reason the NKVD general avoided the young sub captain's eyes at that moment.

'What kind of passengers, Comrade General?' Bogodan asked, innocently enough. 'Military?'

The other man shrugged. 'Perhaps a few soldiers and sailors. Naturally Fritz officers are trying to escape, like rats deserting the sinking ship.'

'And the rest? Other Fritzes?'

The general hesitated. 'There will be some Fritzes, I suppose. They are in the camps, too—'

'*Camps?*' Bogodan asked sharply. 'The Fritz concentration camps?'

'Why, of course. They don't want their victims to fall into our hands, do they?

171

Think of the propaganda we could make of their cruelties if they did.'

Bogodan looked at the other man aghast; he could not believe his own ears. 'But they are the victims of the Fascists, Comrade General. Some of them could be our own people – Russians!'

But the general wasn't listening. His mind was already on vodka and more young virgins, as the door flew open to reveal the wild scene in the big, smoke-filled room. 'Orders are orders,' he snapped coldly, leaving Bogodan standing there, dismayed.

Two

The American struck the kind of pose they had all become accustomed to back in 1942 when the Yanks had first started to come to London on leave in large numbers. In his ragged khaki, he leaned against the wall of the hut, one hand in his pocket, the other holding the precious tailor-made cigarette bought from a guard, his foot supporting his weak legs. To any casual observer he seemed to be staring into nothingness, idly passing the long, boring hours in Stalag VIIIa. For, in truth, most of the prisoners, who were from half a dozen nations, were too weak and emaciated to indulge in any other activity.

Lofty, concealed behind the smashed window of her hut, was listening attentively to the tall, unshaven paratrooper as he briefed her, talking out of the side of his mouth like a Hollywood gangster preparing to escape from the 'stir'.

'A few words of warning first, sister. The

173

goons here were specially selected, when this was a real POW camp. Most of them speak some English and a few of them can lip-read. Even at a distance they can understand what you're saying. Got it?'

Lofty had, but she didn't respond. Out of the corner of her eyes she saw another long column of slow-moving, emaciated prisoners struggling down the coastal road, carrying their pathetic bits and pieces, heading for the port. Ever since dawn they had been doing so, urged on by guards on horseback, armed with whips and rifles. When anyone fell out and the whip didn't bring him to his feet again, the rifle spoke and that was that. The verges on both sides of the road were now littered with the dead.

'There are seismographic devices attached to mikes below the ground to pick up the sound of any tunnelling – they pick up the slightest vibration,' said the Yank, who had warned them to get out of the camp as soon as possible. 'Not that any of us are in a fit state to do any digging. But I'm just warning you in case.'

'Thanks,' she whispered cautiously.

'Be my guest,' the Yank said with an attempt at humour. 'I'll do anything for a white woman – ain't seen many of them since Bastogne.'

She knew what he meant. The Yank had been captured with the 101st US Airborne at the siege of the Belgian town four months before. His cocky manner hadn't pleased his captors, so, instead of being sent to a normal POW camp he had been imprisoned in what he called 'the bad boys' camp'. There, in the Germans' eyes, his behaviour had become worse. In the end he had been transferred to this place that housed those prisoners, men and women, suitable for 'special treatment'.

'You'd better watch that *Hauptmann* Fischer as well,' he continued, still talking out of the side of his mouth. 'He may seem a bit dumb, But he ain't. Just like any other ole schoolteacher, he's got goddam eyes on the back of his head – excuse my French, ma'am,' the Yank added hastily. 'He'll rat on you to the SS and the Gestapo like a shot if he thinks it's to his own advantage and, like the rest of the guards here, he'd sell his own mother to the devil if it saved him from being sent to fight the Russkis.' He paused and watched as one of the guards, a fat little fellow with the face of a pig, started slapping a cavernous giant dressed in the rags of the Red Army. Time and time again, his breath fogging on the cold sea air with the effort, he slammed the Russian's head from side to side, obviously enjoying himself. For his part, the Russian took his punishment stoically until, finally tiring of the exercise, the guard with the pig's face pulled out his pistol and fired a couple of casual shots into the prisoner's chest. He gave a sigh, almost of relief, and went down without another sound. The slow procession of misery wound on.

The Yank said, his tone almost matter-of-fact, 'That's gonna happen to us all, you know. One way or another, the Krauts are going to kill us – we know too much. You, too, ma'am, if you don't do something *soon*.'

'Well, what are *you* going to do?' Lofty whispered from her hiding place behind the shattered window frame.

'Don't know exactly, ma'am. But I'm sure not going to let the bastards kill me without some sort of a fight. Us Screaming Eagles have been taught to die on our feet and not on our knees.' He stopped abruptly. 'Watch it,' he muttered urgently. 'Here comes creeping Jesus himself, *Hauptmann* Fischer. I'm off. I don't want him to spot me talking to you. Bye.' He levered himself from the wall of the hut in that casual, lazy American fashion and staggered off, hands in his pocket, and he didn't salute the ex-school-master as he was supposed to. It would be his last act of defiance.

Hastily Lofty turned to the others loung-
ing on their bunks, dozing yet again, for
their rations had been reduced almost to
nothing in Stalag VIIIa and all of them, even
Rosie, were finding it ever more difficult to
stay on their feet for too long. And just like
the rest, the big-bosomed Scot's periods had
ceased, too. It was a sign, the women knew,
that their physical reserves were about exhausted.

'Goon in the block,' she whispered urgently. 'His nibs – *Hauptmann* Fischer.'

Fischer was happy. The fat quartermaster
in charge of the camp's rations and other
supplies had turned out to be more generous than most of his kind in an emergency
situation. Usually they hung on to their
stores, as if they were their personal possessions, even at the direst of times. Not this
one. He had presented every officer with a
discreet package of wine, cigarettes and
tinned meat, even a small pack of real-bean
coffee, worth a fortune on the black market.
In addition, he had issued a special ration of
pea soup and sausage for breakfast, complete with a bottle of Munich beer. Obviously he, too, was trying to ensure his
future; he wasn't going to be abandoned by
the armed guards to the mercy of the

Russians, who were now only a couple of kilometres away from Stalag VIIIa.

Now Fischer, red-faced with the food and the beer, strode into the hut, clicked his heels together, gave a slight bow from the waist like some gallant cavalry officer, saluted and said, 'Ladies, we march tonight at eighteen hundred hours.'

They looked aghast at the red-faced *Hauptmann*, who smelled strongly of beer. 'March? March where?' Lofty, the first to find her voice, queried. 'Where are we marching?'

Fischer smiled. 'It is a military secret, ladies. But I will tell you. We march to Swinemunde. There we wait for a large ship to cross the Baltic,' he lied glibly. 'There, in Schleswig-Holstein, you will be safe from the Russian swine. They show no respect for women.'

'They are our allies,' Lofty said coldly, though her mind was racing. The hour of decision had come, she realized that. Whatever the future held, one thing was certain. The Germans would attempt to get rid of them. They had all known that, ever since they had been evacuated from their French prisons to this remote German province. They were an embarrassment to the Germans, especially now that they were almost defeated; they would try to get rid of all incriminating evidence.

Hastily she tested him on what their prospects were for the immediate future. '*Herr* Hauptmann, we shall need food for the march. Here we have nothing left to eat. We need something to keep us going on the march.'

Fischer waved his hand vaguely. 'I shall see to it in due course,' he answered, the smile now vanished. 'Now you must prepare for the march.' He clicked his heels together, touched his gloved hand to the tip of his cap, and departed.

Lofty sat down on the wooden bunk, feeling very deflated. Although she had been expecting this to happen all along – the dire knowledge confirmed by what the nameless Yank had just said – now that it had happened she felt completely lost. For the moment her mind seemed completely void of ideas. The others appeared to be in the same boat. They slumped or lay there numbly, with no idea of what to do next. They were starved, just skin and bones, worn down by the months of torture and imprisonment, their minds refusing to function. Indeed, at that particular moment, Lofty felt like simply letting herself go and quietly sobbing. It would be the final relief to do so.

Surprisingly enough it was Jessie, their youngest member, the daughter of a French woman and a World War One Tommy, who had married her and taken her back to the wool mills of the West Riding, who broke that heavy brooding silence. Jessie, the working-class girl who, despite the fact that she had fought off a patrol of the French fascist *Milice* until her ammunition had run out and she had been captured and handed over to the Gestapo, often felt inhibited in the presence of the others.

Now, however, she forgot her inhibitions, knowing that they were all facing imminent death. 'Tha's no use looking laik a wet Monday mornin' in Pontefract,' she exclaimed. 'We've got to do someat, lasses, or we'll never see them white cliffs again.'

Lofty roused herself by an effort of sheer willpower. 'But what do you suggest, Jessie?'

'Nowt really, Lofty. But I'm thinkin' we ought not to let his nibs, that four-eyed bugger, Fischer, tell us what to do. Why should we wait for him to decide what's gonna happen to us?'

'You mean, Jessie,' Lofty said slowly, an idea beginning to uncoil in her mind like a slow snake, 'get on with it before he turns up at six?'

'Aye, someat like that. Yon Jerry thinks he's

got us taped. We'll do anything he sez. But there ain't no law that sez we should, is there, lasses?'

There was a murmur of agreement and Lofty stroked her sharp chin thoughtfully.

It was just after they shot the Yank paratrooper on the wire that Lofty knew she had a rough-and-ready solution. Perhaps the shock of seeing the young American slowly die did it. The fact that *Hauptmann* Fischer, even more drunk now, directed the soldiers who were taking pot shots at the dying man hastened her decision. It certainly increased the fury and determination of the women not to allow themselves to be slaughtered like dumb animals.

It was, therefore, accepted by all as the only possible solution when she announced what they were going to do. 'We're going out with the others from the big compound.' She indicated the groups of some 250 men and women who had been forming up to be marched to the coast all afternoon. 'I know they're under guard, too. But the guards don't know them from Adam. If we wait till six, Fischer, the bastard, will know exactly who *we* are. There'll be no chance of our escaping, girls, and I don't need to draw you a picture of what he intends to do with us.' She pointed to the Yank paratrooper, dead at last, hanging from the wire, arms outstretched, head bloody where it rested on the cruel prongs of the barbed wire like some latterday Christ on the cross.

There was a sad murmur of assent and Nellie Dean, the devout Catholic, crossed herself. The decision had been made. Now the problem was how to carry it out and get away with it. Slowly it was beginning to get dark and, over at the quartermaster stores the drunken supply people were handing out more and more bottles to the equally drunk guards. The time had come to make the break.

Three

Dawn. Slaughter knew he was taking a risk passing through the straits that led to the exit from the inland lake at this time of day. Even though they had camouflaged the skimmers again with branches and sods of grass so that they looked like large bundles of driftwood, any acute observer on either bank would recognize the craft for what they really were. Slaughter, however, was banking on the fact that dawn was the time when it was usual in most armies to change lookouts and sentries. He reasoned the ones going off duty would be too tired and too eager to get to their breakfasts and their bunks to pay much attention to what was happening on the water, while those coming on duty would still be rubbing the sleep out of their eyes and would not be too attentive – yet. At least, that's what the tough SBS officer was banking on.

All the same, the full complement of SBS troopers were now on alert. Hidden among foliage, they manned their machine guns and rifles, ready for action at a moment's notice. As Slaughter had instructed them an hour before, when they had had their last brew-up before setting off again, 'Don't mess about. If the balloon goes up, lads, hammer the buggers with all you've got. Keep 'em away from their own weapons and then we'll go all out and the devil take the hindmost.'

Spiv had responded in a solemn tone, folding his hands as if in prayer, 'For what we are about to receive, let the Lord make us truly grateful.' No one had laughed.

Now they were almost there. Before the exit they could just make out the white comb of the breakers where the Baltic broke against the white sand on the beach. But Slaughter and his troopers had no eyes for the beauty of that Baltic beach. Their gaze flew from one side of the exit to the other. To starboard there was Usedom, set back a little from the coast. To port they could make out the large village of Anklam, and they could see from the smoke rising stiffly into the still, dawn sky that the locals – and probably the garrison too – were already awake and going about their business. Slaughter told himself that it might be a good sign. The Russians were getting closer.

184

Perhaps the locals were already packing and getting ready to flee, too preoccupied with their own safety to worry about what was happening on the water to their front. He hoped so, at least. 'Reduce speed,' he ordered Williams, who was at the control. 'Let's try to keep the wake to a minimum.'

'Yessir.'

Number One skimmer slowed down even more. Even those on deck could barely hear the engine. They hoped that the enemy wouldn't either. Behind them the telltale white wake vanished. Now it was almost as if they were drifting – a mass of foliage brought down by some storm, perhaps. Slaughter licked his lips, which were suddenly very dry. At his right temple a vein started to tick nervously. He knew the signs. It didn't matter how many times you had been in action, you could never overcome the nervous tension of waiting for that first angry challenge, the sudden flare, the harsh, dry crack of the first bullet being fired at you by some unknown enemy soldier.

They came closer and closer to the exit. Somewhere a bugle was being blown, a fine, sweet note. Perhaps it was reveille for the garrison. The noise started a dog barking hysterically attempting to guard whatever property they found themselves beside.

Despite the coldness of the morning, with a fresh, light breeze coming off the sea, Slaughter could feel the cold sweat trickling down the small of his back.

Now the tense troopers could make out the individual buildings on either side of the exit. They were the half-timbered type with straw roofs typical of the area. But here and there were newer ones made of red brick, which could be official structures built for the new German army and navy back in the mid-thirties. Slaughter resisted the temptation to survey them with his binoculars. A glint of glass from inside what was supposed to be a pile of floating foliage might well give the game away. Still he concentrated his gaze on these newer buildings.

But when the trouble came, it did so from a totally different and unexpected quarter: the air. Suddenly, startlingly, a Fiesler Storch, the German reconnaissance plane, came zooming up from beyond Anklam, rose high into the sky and then seemed to stop in mid-air right above the two camouflaged skimmers. Even before the firing commenced, a sickened Slaughter knew that they had been spotted. They had. Almost instantly from port side, there came the sudden chatter of a heavy machine gun like the sound of an angry woodpecker.

186

White tracer zipped across the still water, increasing speed by the instant as it got closer to the two skimmers.

Slaughter opened his mouth to shout an order, but he didn't need to. Spiv in Number One skimmer tucked the butt of his Bren gun more snugly into his right shoulder and pressed the trigger, yelling, 'Try this one on for size, you Jerry sod!'

The Bren erupted into fire. Tracer – red and green now – sped towards where Spiv had spotted the enemy machine gun. In that same instant, Corporal Young opened up. The skimmer throbbed with urgent energy. Its bow tilted upwards. Slaughter felt a sudden breeze slap him in the face. The Storch that had spotted them circled and descended. Slaughter knew what the pilot was about. He was spotting for the gunners on both sides of the exit and, even as he raised his Sten gun to fire at the plane – which was flying at almost stalling speed – he knew that it wouldn't be more than seconds before the German heavy guns, directed by the pilot, opened up at them, and in the narrow confines of the exit they were sitting ducks. He groaned to himself. Things were falling apart rapidly.

There was a roar like a huge piece of canvas being torn apart. A flat crack. To their front a huge fountain of whirling white water erupted furiously. Slaughter's heart sank. There was no mistaking that bloody sound. It was that of the feared 88mm German cannon. The enemy had turned the 88s – normally used as flak – into their ground role, with shells that could penetrate the thickest armour of enemy tanks. What chance did their frail skimmers stand?

Again the plane came in low. The pilot now started to drop flares over the skimmers, as Williams and Young increased their speed to escape the shelling. Slaughter reacted immediately. The flares dropped by the Storch would act as a better indicator for the German gunners than any radio signal could. He raised his Sten gun. Without seeming to take aim, he pressed the trigger of the cheap little machine pistol. Fortunately there was no stoppage, as there often was with the flimsy weapon. A stream of 9mm slugs zipped into the sky. They ripped the Storch's engine apart. An abrupt splutter. A throaty cough. A cloud of oily-black smoke. Then the engine caught again. New power flooded it. Not for long. Slaughter caught a glimpse of the pilot's frantically contorted face as he tried to keep the little plane airborne. To no avail. He sensed the pilot screaming as he lost

188

control. Then the Storch was falling out of the sky, trailing evil black smoke behind it. With a great splash it hit the water. The cockpit crumpled. Slaughter caught one last look of the pilot and then the plane disappeared, carried to the bottom of the inland sea with the force of the impact.

Spiv cheered and cried, 'That'll serve the bugger right!' But the cry of triumph died on his lips. For in that same moment the 88mm cannon roared again and this time the German gunners didn't miss. Behind them Number Two Skimmer disappeared in a ball of angry orange fire. One moment it was there, the next it had disintegrated totally to vanish in a mess of broken wood and metal and the headless body of Staff Sergeant Williams floating stupidly among the wreckage.

'Oh my God!' Young quavered and for one fleeting instant an alarmed Slaughter thought he was going to lose control altogether. 'Stand fast there,' he started to say, but the young SBS volunteer caught hold of himself just in time. He had already somehow learned the hard lesson of the fighting soldier. You must abandon seriously wounded comrades when they compromise the mission, for the mission was everything.

Hastily Slaughter pushed Young to one

side and took over the controls of the skimmer himself. He knew if they were to escape the German gunners they'd need every bit of his experience in the Med to pull it off. Now he opened the throttle full out. The skimmer leaped forward. Hastily Young grabbed for support. To the rear the others opened up blindly. At that speed they couldn't aim. A hail of tracer sped towards the shore, with Spiv and the rest hoping their fire might put off the German gunners or rattle them till they reached the protection of the land beyond the exit.

But Slaughter still had a trick up his sleeve. Already a bright-red light was winking on the shore, indicating the German gunners had not been put off by the bursts of machine-gun fire. They were firing once again. Next moment he knew they were once again getting dangerously close to the flying skimmer. Their very next shell would definitely hit them, he cursed as the huge shell plunged into the water a mere twenty yards away, throwing up a great spout of water that came showering down on the skimmer, making it rock wildly to left and right, as if it were a child's boat on some English lake caught by a sudden gust of wind. He flung a glance to his front. The exit was some hundred or so yards away.

Soldiers were running along the landspit, unslinging their rifles as they ran.

'Bastard!' he cursed again and then pulled the only trick left to him.

With his free hand, balancing himself against the wildly swaying deck, he pulled the trigger of the smoke dischargers. A sharp click. A soft plop. The tiny bombs rose high into the air to either side of the speeding craft. Next moment they had exploded in a stream of thick grey smoke and then Slaughter couldn't see anything to his front. He'd have to steer blindly.

Again, the great 88mm crashed into action. But this time the German gunners were off-target. The shell slammed into the water way behind the flying skimmer and as the little smokescreen started to part to Slaughter's front, he could see that he had already reached the exit and the soldiers waiting for them on the landspit, weapons at the ready.

But the German infantry, confident that *they* couldn't miss even if the *Luftwaffe* gunners on the other shore had, were in for a surprise. They hadn't reckoned with the combat-wise SBS troopers. Now they approached ever closer to the landspit, the 88mm cannon no longer firing for they were now in its 'dead ground'. Spiv and the rest prepared their little surprise for the German infantry.

A fat officer, still wearing his pyjama top and carpet slippers, raised his hand as if in signal. His men clicked back the bolts of their Mausers. He dropped his hand and yelled, *'Feuer!'* A volley erupted the length of the spit. Bullets ripped the length of the flying skimmer. Wood splintered. The little makeshift radio serial came tumbling down in a flurry of angry blue sparks. The perspex glass in front of the little bridge splintered into a glittering spider's web. Spiv yelped with pain as a slug sliced the flesh off his shoulder.

The fat officer yelled in triumph. But his triumph was short-lived. Now a cursing Spiv and the rest brought their only real offensive weapon into action. It was a small hand-held two-inch mortar. In the same instant that the Germans clicked their bolts to fire another volley, the loader dropped the little mortar bomb down the tube, yelling 'Fire!' and Spiv, grasping the base, despite the blood spurting a bright-red from his wound, turned the firing wheel smartly. There was an obscene thud. The winged bomb rose high in the sky. A moment later it came hurtling down right on to where the fat officer stood and exploded in an angry flash of flame. The fat officer disappeared, as if he had never existed. All that was left of him was his helmet, complete with head, rolling slowly towards the water like a football abandoned by some careless child. A second or two later the lone skimmer was through and heading at a crazy pace for the open sea. They were in the Baltic.

Four

On the quayside, stained yellow with the droppings and urine of the skinny-ribbed horses that carried supplies for the Red Navy to and fro, burly old *babushkas* wrapped up in heavy shawls were filleting the latest catch of herring, chanting a song all the while. Here and there were skinny men in leather coats, who should have been in the services, watching the sailors come and go, laden with their kitbags and equipment. They were obviously pimps who had bribed doctors to free them from military service. Grouped behind them, as though waiting for any scraps or cigarette ends that the pimps might give them, were the war cripples: veterans of the Red Army's four years of war, legless, armless, some wearing the armband and dark glasses of the war-blinded. Now that they could no longer fight, the State had abandoned them. They received a pitiful pension and whatever they could beg on the docks.

Bogodan frowned. Leningrad had once been the richest city in Russia. Now it couldn't afford to ensure that its citizens who had given their blood for Mother Russia enjoyed a decent basic standard of living. It wasn't right, Bogodan knew that, but one day it would all be rectified, he was certain. People like himself would ensure it was. They would clear away the corruption and abuse of the system that those one-time revolutionaries and now old men, whose main concern was the preservation of their privileges, had introduced.

For a moment he recalled the soulful Soviet song he had learned as a young Pioneer before the war. 'Your Motherland lies deep inside you and no one or nothing can take it away from you.' That was true, no one could take away his Motherland, nor would he allow them to do so if they ever tried. He took one last look at the River Neva and the great eighteenth-century buildings, now shattered ruins left by the great three-year siege. But first that would have to be avenged, he told himself, and then, when the Great Patriotic War was done, he and those like him would deal with the enemy within.

The staff car came to a stop. He collected his valise and his secret orders and strode purposefully to the sentries guarding the entrance to the submarine pens. They clicked to attention when they saw his rank and his chestful of polished medals that he always bore when he boarded his sub. The men liked the ceremony, the precision, polish and cleanliness of that first day. For soon they'd be bearded, unwashed, pasty-faced creatures who stank to high heaven after days inside the tight confines of the sub, which smelled of men's odours and their constant breaking of wind.

The men in their best uniforms, too, were lined up on the deck. A band played as it always did when a submarine sailed on a mission. At periodic intervals, a guard of honour of young cadets, most of them not yet fourteen, raised their clenched fists in the Communist salute and barked in unison, '*Slava Krasnaya Flotte*!'

Bogodan smiled. This really was the new Russia. The smart crew, most of them not much older than the cadets in their blue uniforms, the band playing its patriotic marches, the eager, red-faced cadets. This was what it was all about.

He started to ascend the gangplank. Piotr, his second-in-command, an old comrade among all the new faces of the replacements, stood at the top waiting to receive him. The former winked, allowing himself the privileges of an old shipmate. Hastily Bogodan winked back and then, with his face solemn, his right hand raised in salute, he stepped onboard as the petty officer commanded in a shout that set the gulls off rising in squawking protest, 'Captain, prepare for inspection.'

Bogodan, hand still raised in salute, followed by Piotr, walked slowly down the ranks of his young sailors, all volunteers for the submarine service, staring hard at each face as if trying to etch it on his mind's eye forever. That finished, he called to the senior petty officer to stand the crew at ease. Without wasting any time, Bogodan launched into his little speech. 'I shall not waste words, comrades,' he said. 'Our mission is vital for the future of the Fatherland. It will be carried out at all costs. It is the Little Father's specific order.' There was a gasp of surprise when he made mention of the dictator Stalin's name. Bogodan didn't appear to notice. 'There will be dangers, I can assure you of that. We shall overcome them in the name of our Soviet Fatherland. Comrades, we sail on the tide.' He raised his voice. 'Chief Petty Officer!'

'Comrade Captain?'

'Dismiss the men to their stations.' Half an

hour later they were on their way...

'Well, comrades,' Bogodan announced as he squatted in the tight, fetid confines of his skipper's cabin, together with Piotr and Igor, the Engineering Officer. 'This is what we have, as you, Igor, already know.' He nodded at the burly bearded officer. 'Three T8 killer-destroyer torpedoes. The experts tell me they will revolutionize submarine warfare.'

'How?' Piotr asked in that direct manner of his.

'Because the T8 is battery-driven so that it leaves no telltale wake to alert the enemy of what is coming to stick them right up the arse.' Bogodan was no friend of the coarseness of the average submariner's language, but he knew such expressions relieved tension and so he used them now and again.

Igor grinned, tugged at his beard and said, '*Horoscho*,' as if the explanation had eradicated all his worries. But then, as Bogodan knew, Igor really was only concerned with his engines; his whole life seemed to centre on them.

'There is one other thing,' he continued. 'They home in on their target. They've tried them out in Leningrad. On Lake Lagoda. They used a fast patrol boat, belting around at thirty-odd knots an hour, and the patrol boat simply couldn't shake the T8.' Bogodan looked at his two officers, his face very serious. 'Once the T8 is launched and locks on to its target, there is no hope for that target. It simply can't escape, especially if it's a nice fat liner with no speed or manoeuvrability to speak off.'

Igor, as sharp as ever, caught the words 'nice fat liner' immediately. 'Is that what we're after, Bogodan?' he snapped quickly. 'A nice fat liner?'

The skipper hesitated. He had been ordered not to tell the crew what they were going after, but it would be impossible to hide the kind of target they were aiming for from his two officers. 'Let me say this, friends,' he said quietly. 'What I will tell you now, and what in due course you will see and experience, must remain a secret. You risk – well, you know what you risk, don't you, if you blab.' Even as he said the words, Bogodan felt a sense of guilty outrage that he must threaten his own officers into secrecy when they were risking their lives for the Fatherland. Such things should not happen in modern Russia. They were patriots just as he was. Why should the authorities make them fear for their life to make them do what they were prepared to do anyway?

He dismissed the problem, which had

agitated him for months, and said, 'Yes, a liner. It will be bigger than the *Wilhelm Gustloff*. You remember?'

The other two nodded that they did. 'Which?' Igor asked eagerly. 'There can't be many Fritz ships bigger than the *Gustloff*.'

'I don't know, though I might guess. Once we are in position off the Pomeranian coast, we shall be informed from which of those German ports it will be sailing. Moscow tells me we have agents in every one of—'

He never finished his explanation, for at that moment there came an urgent whistling down the speaking-tube that led directly from the bridge to his tiny cabin. Hastily he picked up the tube, whistled down it and held it up to his ear. *'Da, gavorit!'* he commanded.

'Comrade Captain. Boat to starboard, comrade.'

'What kind of boat?' he asked impatiently.

'Looks like a dinghy or small fishing boat. It's got no power. Riding on the waves.'

Bogodan grabbed for his cap. 'I'll go up top at once.'

Balanced in the conning tower together with men on watch, Bogodan focused his glasses on the boat bobbing up and down on the waves a little helplessly as the stiff breeze from the east whipped them up into a white fury. He adjusted the focus and caught a glimpse of half a dozen or so wretched men huddled behind the gunwhale trying to protect themselves from the icy water that swept over the side every time the boat reeled. 'German?' he asked no one in particular, for they were well within the part of the Baltic that was controlled by the enemy.

Next to him, Igor focused his glasses and replied, 'Nyet, Tovarisch. Well, they're not in German uniform, at least. They're in some sort of striped gear, poor bastards.'

Bogodan caught his breath. He knew what that striped gear was. He had seen those emaciated wretches in similar striped uniform when he had been called to see the NKVD general at the inn in newly conquered East Prussia. 'They might be escapees from a concentration camp!' he exclaimed. 'Helmsman, steer a course on them.' He bent his head to the conning tower speaking-tube, which linked him to the engine room where Igor was again in command. 'Both ahead, Comrade Engineer,' he ordered. 'Slow.'

Very slowly, the submarine moved forward. Bogodan didn't want to make too much of a bow wave. The little boat with the helpless civilians aboard was almost swamped as it was. Behind him, Piotr ordered, 'Board watch ... ready with the hooks.' He had outguessed the skipper. The submarine would have to anchor the little craft securely to its own side if they wanted to question the strangers. At the same time they didn't want to be attached to it by hawsers just in case some damned long-range Focke-Wulfe bomber came falling out of the sky. The sub had to be able to submerge in a matter of seconds at the first sighting of an enemy plane.

Now they were close enough to see the craft more clearly. It had obviously been involved in some kind of fight. Its timbers were splintered and there was a whole line of bullet holes along the bow where a dead man lay sprawled, arms raised towards heaven in a mockery of some saint asking for God's mercy.

'*Sto*?' Bogodan clapped his hands around his mouth and cried. '*Sto*?'

To his surprise a wan figure with cropped hair raised himself above the gunwhale, tried to assume the position of attention, but failed lamentably and answered in Russian, '*Russkiya*? ... Soldiers of the Red Army.'

Piotr flung Bogodan a warning look. They had been told over the radio time and time again that there were traitors, defeatists and other renegades who had betrayed Mother Russia after being captured by the Fritzes and had gone over to the German side. Such men would be punished severely once they fell into the hands of the victorious Red Army.

But Bogodan ignored the warning. He cried, 'What are you doing here? What do you want?'

His words seemed to rouse the men in the sinking boat from their miserable lethargy. Rising from behind the gunwhale like grey ghosts from the grave, they called back weakly, 'Save us, comrade officer ... We have escaped from German slavery ... We are starving.' They held up their skinny claws in a gesture of supplication.

'Comrade Captain,' Piotr tried again as Bogodan ordered the sub to close up completely with the other craft prior to taking the pathetic wretches aboard, 'don't do it—'

'Be silent!' Bogodan cut him short. 'I know what I'm doing. These are honest Russians who have suffered terribly at the hands of the Fritzes. They must be helped.'

Piotr bit his lip and fell silent, but he looked worried. He knew the skipper well enough by now. He was brave and ruthless in combat, showing no mercy to the Fritzes. But he believed in the future and a more honourable and just Russia, and that was a recipe for disaster in a Russia ruled by Stalin.

Hastily Bogodan bent to the voice tube. 'Galley,' he ordered, *'Kleba* ... vodka ... *davoi.'*

Down below the cook gathered together the bread, vodka and water that the skipper had ordered, reaching for the salt, too, in case Bogodan wanted to honour these escapees from the Fritz camps with the traditional Russian bread and salt.

But just as he was about to order the engine room to stop the engines, there was a cry of alarm from the lookout on the fore-deck. 'Red one hundred ... Plane approaching, Comrade Captain.'

Urgently, Piotr flung up his glasses. There was no mistaking the shape that slid into the circle of calibrated glass. There were no Russian planes of that size with four engines. 'Focke-Wulfe Condor, Comrade Captain! And she's coming in for the attack!'

The long-range German reconnaissance bomber was indeed coming down rapidly, her bomb-bays sliding open as the pilot spotted the Russian submarine, almost motionless on the surface of the sea. This was going to be an easy kill.

Bogodan was in a quandary for a moment. On the boat, only a few metres away now, the exhausted escapees were attempting to clamber over the side ready to be taken aboard the submarine, some of them with tears of joy and gratitude streaming down their emaciated faces. After years of imprisonment, starvation and brutality they were at last going home to Mother Russia. Could he really just leave them like that? Should he order them to attempt to swim to the sub? Then he might save the poor swine.

'*Captain ... Bogodan!*' Piotr yelled desperately. 'Think of the sub ... The mission ... *Boshe moi* ... The mission!'

Bogodan acted. 'Clear the bridge,' he commanded as the roar of the Condor's four engines grew in intensity. '*Dive ... Dive ... Dive!*' The klaxon shrilled its urgent warning and then they were sinking below the surface, tears streaming down the young captain's face and the fugitives abandoned to their terrible fate.

Five

It had been easier, much easier, than Lofty had thought it would be. The reason was obvious. The Germans were losing their nerve rapidly. Discipline and the vaunted German efficiency were being thrown out of the window, especially now as the first Russian Sturmovik dive-bombers were appearing off the coast and starting to strafe coastal shipping. Weary and demoralized German infantry were streaming back from the front as well, some without their weapons and all broken in spirit. It woudn't be long before the vanguard of the Red Army made its appearance and the remaining camp guards knew it. They wanted to be out of this dread place of mass murder before the Ivans arrived; they knew only too well what their fate would be if they didn't escape before then. So they were no longer as scrupulous as they had once been. Nervous and drunk for the most part, they formed up the blocks of emaciated, sick wretches who were to be taken to the coast and hurried them on their way without any kind of identity check. Even Captain Fischer, who made an appearance every now and again, seemed little concerned by who was leaving the camp. Indeed he was ready to clear out as soon as he dare. His servant had filled his little Opel Wanderer automobile with his cases, containing the loot he had accumulated from his doomed charges over the years, and was already gunning the engine ready to move at a moment's notice. Besides, the ex-schoolmaster's face was flushed red with drink and he kept resorting to the silver flask that he had previously concealed in the pocket of his greatcoat. But now he didn't care who saw him.

'He'll piss himself now,' Rosie said as they lined up with another batch of men and women waiting for the order to move out, 'and it couldn't happen to a nicer person. The pompous prick.'

Lofty pretended to be shocked. 'Watch your language, Rosie,' she chided her, adding in a whisper, 'And don't talk so much English. We don't want even this lot,' she indicated her fellow prisoners, 'to know who we are. They could shop us, too.'

But no one was in the position or mood to shop them – or anyone else for that matter.

Already, on the hillside beyond, they could see the retiring German infantry digging in, while Panther tanks took up their positions in the fir trees, waiting for the Russians to appear above the ridge. Lofty knew little about military tactics, but she guessed this was going to be the Germans' last line of defence. Once it was broken, the Russians would swoop down on the camp.

There was another worry, too: if the Russians broke through to the coast before they were clear, what would happen to them? She knew from what she had heard that the Russians raped anything in a skirt, whatever their nationality, allied or enemy. But in the women's case, they were also members of the British Intelligence Service. If *they* fell into Russian hands, their erstwhile allies might want to know more about them than their bodies. She clicked her tongue in irritation. She would deal with that eventuality if and when it arose. For the time being, she had to get her girls, as Lofty thought of them, out of the camp before the Germans started the liquidation process – she couldn't bring herself to use the more drastic term.

Half an hour later they were on their way, the drunken guards urging them on with whips and clubs, beating those who lagged

208

behind mercilessly. For the Germans were fearful that the Russians would catch up with them before they reached the protection of the coast, where there were still infantry and able-bodied members of the *Kriegsmarine* who would be able to put up some kind of defence. Behind them the Red Army's leading units were advancing relentlessly. In vain the last-ditch defenders attempted to keep them from their strongpoints and ambush positions. But the advancing Red Army men brooked no hindrance. *'Urrah!'* they would cry and come on in solid ranks, bayonets at the ready, shoulder to shoulder, drunk or drugged, dying by the scores as they advanced into the German machine-gun fire with the next rank plodding over the writhing bodies of their comrades to meet the same fate, but advancing all the while. Overhead the fat-bellied little Yak fighters wheeled and turned, looking for targets, falling out of the sky whenever they spotted a German position, cannon and machine guns thumping crazily. This was an army that didn't count the costs in manpower and material. This was an army that demanded victory at any price. There was no stopping the Russians now.

It was this realization that made Lofty ever

more concerned to keep her girls moving at the head of the column. She knew the guards would lose their nerve sooner or later. Then they'd start shooting the laggards and the stragglers who were slowing them down. At the same time she knew, too, that once the Russians did make their appearance, the guards would panic and make a run for it. Then she and the rest of the girls would have to be ready to take instant cover until the massacre – which it would certainly become – was over. As weary as she was, she now searched the area to her front for that hiding place in an emergency.

But it seemed fate was against her and the girls. They weren't going to escape the clutches of their captors that easily. Someone must have reported their disappearance to the special compound. For now there were German guards on their sturdy little ponies, flogging the creatures' rumps with their whips, galloping down from the abandoned camp, crying urgently, 'The English bitches – they've escaped! Where are the English?'

The prisoners panicked. Most of them probably didn't understand German, but by now they knew the Germans. The mounted guards hurrying after them were intent on killing them. The prisoners had thought they were finally to escape the brutal misery of the concentration camp. But it seemed that wasn't to be. They'd heard ugly rumours about these roadside massacres. Now it was going to happen to them. As emaciated, weary and downtrodden as they were, their will to survive surfaced once more. They broke ranks. Screaming, pushing and jostling each other in their overwhelming fear, they streamed into the fields to left and right, dropping their pathetic bundles, mothers even abandoning their children, leaving them standing trembling in the road, crying bitterly and yelling for their mothers in half a dozen European languages.

As sensitive as she was, Lofty's heart might well have broken at the sight of those abandoned children in their dirty rags. Not now, however. She knew she had her duty to her own children – the girls. Desperately she looked around for some place to hide. Then she had it. She remembered the advice the master of her local hunt had given her as a girl when she had first started to ride to the hounds. 'Never enter a wood on a horse, my dear, if you can avoid it. Woods are full of unexpected dangers for inexperienced horsewomen.'

'Into those trees, girls!' she yelled frantically as the riders came thundering down the hill, riding the fugitives down mercilessly. 'Get into those firs – *quick*!'

'Why?' Jessie protested.

Lofty cut her short. 'Bloody well do as you're told. Run!'

They ran. Their weakness now forgotten, they pelted for all they were worth, arms working like pistons, heading for the protection of the tightly packed fir trees on the hillside to the right like a regiment of spike-helmeted Prussian grenadiers. But already the few leading horsemen had spotted them. *'Da druben*!' they cried. 'They're over there!' Tugging cruelly at the bits of the ponies' muzzles, they forced their mounts round and came on again, heading straight after the fleeing women.

'Scatter!' Lofty cried hurriedly. 'Scatter, girls!'

Back in England they had been trained well, taught how to obey orders instantly and without question. Now they did as she said, parting from each other, each girl heading for a particular break in the lines of the firs. Behind them the guards urged their mounts to greater efforts. They lashed their rumps mercilessly. They dug their heels into the ponies' flanks till the foam burst in great

212

bubbles along their muzzles. But the girls were winning. They'd make it, Lofty knew that. But what then? Like some top-class runner breasting the winning tape, she burst into the firs. She did not stop. Nor did the others. Lungs creaking like those of some ancient asthmatic in the throes of a final attack, they continued to blunder through the tightly packed trees, ignoring the branches that whipped them across the face cruelly, stumbling and slipping on the roots. But they did not stop. They continued their wild flight. For behind them the frustrated guards, who could not force their ponies to enter the forest, were unslinging their rifles, dropping to the ground and taking up the pursuit on foot. Now they were shouting to each other in order to keep in touch as they split up stalking their intended victims, rifles held at the ready, murder in their hearts.

But there were others in the forest, just as wild and rapacious as the guards, and with murder in their hearts, too. The handful of Cossacks – dark, bearded men with their fur hats tilted in the usual rakish fashion – had seen the great trek of unfortunates in their striped pyjamas leaving the camp, but had felt there were too many guards for them to attack, kill and loot whatever they could carry with them and steal a few of the better-shaped women for their pleasure this evening. Instead they had tethered their horses and spread out at the edge of the forest to observe and report to headquarters, which was their job as members of the Black Cossacks' Divisional Reconnaissance.

Now the guards, it seemed, were playing into their hands, and there were women involved too. Who they were and why they were running away from the German guards didn't interest the Cossacks. They were women and once they'd opened their legs, it wouldn't matter who or what they were, they'd give pleasure to men. That was the important thing.

So the Cossacks waited in the undergrowth. A few still carried the curved sabres of their homeland, but most were armed with the Red Army's tommy gun, ideal for the kind of close-quarter fighting that would soon commence. Unlike most troops, they weren't nervous about what was to come. Their race had been brought up to live short, exciting, brutal lives and die young in battle. It was the Black Cossacks' way of life.

The *Hetman*, their leader – a tall, dark-faced giant, his jet-black beard parted in the middle and plaited at the ends – spotted the first of the guards emerging from the firs to his right. He gave the bird-call, their usual signal. Silently his men turned to face the enemy. Another guard came into view and then another. The *Hetman* smiled evilly. What easy meat these Fritzes were.

Now he counted off the metres as the guards, thinking that they were simply looking for a bunch of English 'miladies' who were unarmed and totally harmless, walked straight into the trap. The *Hetman* licked his fat red lips in anticipation of the slaughter to come. *Twenty-five metres* ... The Fritzes were close enough. Even cross-eyed Boris, the worst shot in the detachment – perhaps even in the whole Black Cossack Division – couldn't miss at this range. He raised his gleaming silver sabre, the mark of a *Hetman*, and yelled joyously, 'Fire!'

The slaughter commenced.

Six

They caught Nellie Dean, the devout Catholic, first. Indeed the Cossacks caught her *because* she was such a devout Catholic, praying on her knees, hands clasped together, hidden among a grove of firs, but revealing her position by the volume of her frightened pleas to God in heaven. But that God was looking the other way this terrible early-April day.

There were two of them, already drunk on the potent schnapps they had looted from the bodies of the dead Germans. She tried to rise, but they were quicker. The bigger of the two, a scar-faced youth with one eye – the other had been shot out at Stalingrad –grabbed her by the leg and pulled her down to the ground once more. Even before she hit it, he was ripping down her striped trousers, feeling for the skinny, naked body beneath. Meanwhile his comrade, older and more experienced in such matters, grabbed her shoulders with his big hard hands and held her firmly in his grasp while his young comrade fumbled with his flies.

Desperately Nellie wriggled and turned, trying to avoid what was to come, her nostrils full of the stink of black tobacco, male sweat, schnapps and sex. To no avail. The older man held her in an iron grip. Suddenly the man was ready. He grunted something in his own language. She screamed. It felt as if a red-hot poker was being thrust into her dried-up body. She screamed again. The man holding her shoulders slapped her hard. She saw stars. For a moment she thought she was going to black out, but that wasn't to be. With a high-pitched groan, his whole body quivering as if he had suddenly been seized by a fever, the younger man fell from her and lay panting at her side. The pressure on her shoulders relaxed. But only for a moment, then a heavier body descended upon her. The Cossack said something in Russian. She didn't understand. The man slapped her face, making it move from side to side. *'Komm Frau,'* he commanded thickly in German. *'Mach ... Davoi!'*

She opened her eyes. The older man was leering down at her. Abruptly he bent and took the nipple of her shrivelled breast into his lips. He bit hard. She screamed shrilly.

That seemed to excite him. '*Horoscho!*' he cried and then, as if he were riding one of his steeds, he thrust himself deep inside her, whooping crazily as he did so.

Ten yards or so away, Lofty, her face contorted with horror, fought against the urge to clasp her hands over her ears to drown out the pitiful cries of the tortured woman writhing on the ground between the two Cossacks. That wasn't the way. She had to act, not play the weak woman and try to blot out what was happening to her friend only yards away.

On top of Nellie, the older Cossack felt satisfied and dropped, exhausted into the grass, gasping and panting as if he had just run a long race. But already the younger one was erect again. Holding his penis in front of him as though it were a policeman's truncheon, he used it to nuzzle between Nellie's legs, from which bright-red blood now seeped on to the wrinkled flesh.

Lofty gasped with horror. He was going to rape the poor tortured girl yet again. Her horror turned into a burning rage. What right had these men to take and abuse her friend like this? She knew she must act, cost what it may. She sought and found the razor blade she had hidden for so long. She had kept it to ensure that this final indignity would not be heaped upon herself. Now she'd use it to save her friend.

Hardly knowing what she was doing, she crept forward, the blade held in a hand that trembled slightly. The two Cossacks didn't hear her. They were too concerned with their victim, who was sobbing wildly now, her skinny, abused body racked with pain and shame. Already the older man was clutching his limp organ, trying to make it tumescent for another attempt at rape. Meanwhile the younger man was thrusting himself savagely into Nellie's loins, teeth bared like a madman, gasping wildly, his head thrust back, his hairy throat exposed, concerned solely with the satisfaction of his filthy lusts.

Her hatred of these brutal creatures overcame any fear that Lofty might have felt. She, too, was now consumed by a burning desire to hurt: Rage flamed up within her. She felt like a wild creature herself. Only revenge could quell her hatred and rage. Now she was within striking distance. The two Cossacks had still not become aware of her presence. She had to strike before they did so. She reached out with her free hand. She grasped and pulled the younger Cossack's thick mop of black curls. He gasped something, not pausing in his wild thrusting. She hesitated no longer. With all her strength she drew the sharp blade across his exposed throat. Instantly she felt the hot blood well up and swamp her hand. She exerted more pressure, digging the slippery blade in even deeper. The Cossack's spine arched like a bow. His scream was muffled by his own blood flooding his throat. Desperately he tried to shake Lofty off. In vain. With one last burst of strength, she slashed that killing blade down again. The Cossack gave a last gasp. Next moment he slumped across Nellie's body, dead.

Now, before the other Cossack could really become aware of what was happening, the other women descended upon him. Like a pack of wild animals they attacked him in primeval fury. They beat, tore, scratched, hacked, and finally used his own sword to plunge the blade into his unconscious body and finish him off.

For what seemed a long time afterwards, but could only have been a matter of seconds, they stared down at the dead men and then at each other's vacant faces in blank incomprehension, as if they couldn't understand what they had just done. But then Nellie's moans awoke them to their danger. Lofty, who was verging on hysteria as she realized she had killed a man in cold blood, pulled herself together and hissed, 'Come on, let's get out of here before the others come.'

Rosie, the most practical of them all, said, 'And let's take the bastard's pistol with us.' She indicated the Cossack whose throat Lofty had slit.

No one moved. In the end Rosie pushed him round with her clog and, reaching down, pulled the pistol from his belt. Then she let the dead Cossack fall to the ground once more, saying contemptuously, 'You deserved it, you rapist swine.'

Hastily they pulled a sobbing, bleeding Nellie Dean to her feet and made their way through the forest, pushing blindly through the firs, which lashed their ashen, panicked faces cruelly, knowing nothing but the fact that they must get away from this place of horror and death.

They ran till they could run no more. Behind them the sounds of their hunters died away to be replaced by the sullen rumble of heavy guns as the Russians prepared to make their final attack on the last remaining German line of defence. Broken and gasping crazily, they staggered to a stop, peering through a gap in the forest down to the sea below. The coastal road was packed with vehicles and horse-drawn carts. There were soldiers and civilians too, prisoners like themselves, thrown together indiscriminately, all seeking some kind of safety, though in reality there was none. The only hope lay in the scores of boats and ships moored offshore. They were German civilian and naval craft, all waiting for those they had been ordered to take on board and finally escape to the west.

Now Lofty was imbued with a sudden feeling of hope. She knew that they were still very much in danger, little better than hunted animals. All the same, in that tremendous confusion below, they had a chance. She wiped the sweat from her forehead with a sleeve now caked with dark-red blood. 'Girls, we're going down there. It's our only chance.'

'But they'll be looking for us, Lofty,' Lisa objected. 'And the way we look,' she indicated her ragged clothing, torn and ripped by the trees, 'we'll stand out a mile.'

'I know,' Lofty answered impatiently, wanting to be off now, just in case the Cossack patrol made an appearance again. 'It's a chance we must take. I'm banking on the panic and confusion down there to see us through. I'm guessing that everyone is looking after himself down there.'

'Aye, ye'll be right there,' Rosie said. 'Besides,' she tapped the pistol now hidden beneath the striped jacket, 'none o' yon buggers is gonna take me again, if I can help it. I've had enough of being a bluidy prisoner.'

There was a rumble of agreement from the others and Lofty understood that their escape from the Cossacks and their German pursuers had given the women a new confidence in themselves. She felt the same, too, but as her mother had often said to her as a girl, 'Clarissa, there's many a slip between the cup and the lip in this life. Remember that, my dear.' It wouldn't do to be overconfident. That had been their downfall in France. Now they had finally escaped, but this was their last chance. They couldn't afford to be overconfident and make some fatal mistake this time.

It was for this reason that she made her suggestion as they prepared to leave the forest and join the crowded beach road leading to Swinemunde. 'We'll break up into twos, girls. But we'll keep within a certain distance of each other. It'll give us a better chance than if we went down in a group.'

There was a murmur of agreement from the others and Rosie said, 'Let's pick our partners then for the waltz.'

'Let's hope it ain't the last waltz,' Jessie, the ultimate realist, snorted, but no one was listening to her.

They set off again. Now they were almost on the last leg of their long journey to the freedom they had hoped for these last terrible months. A band of weary, ragged, brave women, whose spirit was almost broken, but who still hoped that fortune would favour them. Minutes later they had disappeared out of sight.

The stage was set, the actors were in place. The last act of the drama could commence...

FOUR

End Run

One

'Shall we scramble now, sir?' Fleming asked, finger poised over the scrambler button of the special red telephone.

'Yes, we can. One moment, Commander,' C answered in that dry-as-dust voice. 'Now,' he pressed his own button in that rooftop office of his in Queen Anne's Gate, 'you may speak.'

'Sir, I thought I'd try to keep you up to date on the situation in the Baltic.'

'Thank you. Please proceed.'

At that moment, Fleming could imagine the chief of the Special Intelligence Service hunched over his desk, face hidden in the shadows and revealing nothing. Once again Fleming wondered for an instant what went on in the mind of the old man who knew where the skeletons were buried – hence his great power. Yet as always, he concluded he hadn't the faintest idea. C was as devious as ever. So he made his report instead. 'Sir, the last we have from the skimmers is that

Slaughter's people were under attack and that one of the skimmers was lost to German fire. Since then we have heard no more from Slaughter. Our radio people here at the Admiralty assumed that either he is maintaining radio silence due to pressure from the enemy or, more probably, that his wireless equipment was hit during the German attack.'

'When did you last hear from this Slaughter chap?'

'Rather in the nature of thirty hours, sir,' Fleming answered dutifully.

For a moment C was silent. 'I see,' he said finally before asking, 'And these SOE women in their camp – what of them?'

'Aerial recce, sir, shows the camps are being evacuated. I imagine by now they will have been evacuated of their prisoners, including the women in question. The Reds are advancing rapidly on that whole area and the Huns are falling back to the coast in the hope of being taken off by their own people and being transported to Schleswig-Holstein. I'm afraid we've been unable to carry out any more aerial reconnaissance since yesterday. RAF Bomber Command informs me that the Russians are attacking our planes as soon as they enter air space controlled by the Red Air Force.'

'Bugger,' C said mildly. 'It's started, you see, Fleming. We're just about to win the war against the Hun and now the Bolshevik is rearing his ugly head again just as he did in 1918, and if nothing is done, we'll be fighting the Reds soon. But no matter,' he said dismissively. 'What is your opinion of the fate of these SOE women?'

Fleming didn't answer at once. He knew the response that C wanted to hear, but how could he give it? So he compromised. 'On the face of it, sir, just like Slaughter and his SBS team, they've had it. I mean, we can't be sure, but my guess in the confused mess that seems to prevail in that part of the world, they're as good as goners.'

C gave a little sigh, which Fleming took to be of satisfaction. 'I hope you're right, Commander. The PM's in one of his moods. He's been snapping at me all damned week. He thinks the SIS is letting him down again on the secret information front. In reality he has no idea what it takes to get that kind of information. In contrast he's full of how well the SOE is doing, with their showy operations in the Far East and the like. Therefore, we don't want these SOE women turning up at this moment in time. The gutter press would have a field day. Our brave women agents and all that tosh, what?'

'What,' Fleming echoed.

'All right, Commander, you can un-scramble now. But please keep me inform-ed. Let us hope, however, that this is the last we've heard of this chap Slaughter and those damned spy women. After all, drop-ping behind enemy lines and all that kind of business … Take it from me, Commander, as an older man, the only place that a woman agent should be operating from is *bed*, on her back, with her legs spread wide, eh?' He chuckled, an eerie sound coming from that dried-up grey man, who appeared to have given up the pleasures of the flesh many years ago. The phone went dead. Fleming turned off his own scrambler switch and replaced his phone on its cradle.

For a moment or two, he reflected on what the crusty old head of the SIS had said, especially his final words about a woman agent operating in bed, on her back, with her legs spread wide. He had liked that and it had set his mind wandering to the little nubile Wren who brought in the coals and his tea in the morning. He had agreed to take her out to lunch this day. Naturally it wouldn't be to one of the better places, where he was known. Besides, it wasn't the done thing for a commissioned officer to be seen dining another rank. He'd have to take her to one of those dago places where they served expensive black-market food. They always had plenty of booze, though. He'd ply her with cheap bubbly; that usually did the trick with the working-class types, and if she didn't play ball, there was always his whip. The thought excited him. He could already visualize her leaning over the sofa in his flat, those pert little buttocks exposed, all white and fetching. My God, he'd soon turn them a bright, stinging red with the lash.

Suddenly very happy and excited he forgot all about those other women, whose fate he guessed was already sealed. For Commander Fleming, who one day would make his living from writing, in part, about female agents operating from a bed with their legs spread wide, they had already become a footnote in the history of World War Two...

'Up came a spider, sat down beside her, whipped his old bazooka out and this is what he said,' the wounded Spiv sang monotonously as he handled the steering as best he could with his one hand, while the others pushed the skimmer deep into the tall reeds that fringed the white dunes of the Baltic shore. *'Get hold o' this, bash-bash. Get hold o' that, bash-bash ... I've got a lovely bunch o' coconuts ... I've got a*

lovely bunch o' balls...'

They had run out of fuel at last and it was damned hard work pushing the craft into the hiding place he had just selected for the skimmer, so – despite the fact that the little cockney SBS trooper was way off-key – Slaughter was glad of his singing. The men needed some cheering up after the loss of Number Two Skimmer and its crew – a loss that wasn't lessened by the knowledge that they had landed on this hostile shore with very little chance, under present circumstances, of getting off again.

'Big ones, small ones, balls as big as yer head.' Spiv continued to sing as the reeds began to hide them from the sea, which seemed to be filled with German shipping of all kinds right up to what looked like pre-war liners, now painted a drab camouflage colour.

Slaughter had recovered from the shock of losing the other skimmer; in these last, terrible years he had lost too many comrades to mourn them for too long. Now he was trying to plan ahead, though at the moment his mind was confused. As far as he could make out, they had beached some five kilometres east of Swinemunde, which was one of the Baltic ports that fed seaborne traffic into Stettin, the major port of that part of the inland sea, hence the amount of traffic

232

they could see behind them at the moment. If they were going to ship the SOE women out into the Baltic, he guessed Swinemunde would be as likely a port of departure as any other. So far, so good. But how were they going to find the missing female agents in the confusion of a German army in retreat, with the SS and Gestapo intent on eliminating the evidence of Germany's war crimes? That was going to be a tough one.

He paused for a moment and wiped the sweat from his forehead. Behind them the spring sky had begun to turn a dull, ominous brown, with patches of scudding cloud. The sea was beginning to break white. Flurries of waves ran inland and broke about the skimmer, making it shake. He could feel the craft vibrate even as he held it. There was a storm in the offing. Slaughter thought it might be to their advantage as it would probably keep people away from the shore.

Spiv didn't think so. He broke off his singing to complain, 'Bloody cold all of a sudden, skipper. Shouldn't be surprised if there ain't snow soon. Heaven help a sailor on a night like this.' He shivered dramatically.

Slaughter forced a grin. The storm might well provide the cover they needed. All the same, his hard-pressed men needed shelter, warmth and, above all, food. As their fuel had come to an end, so had their compo rations. Even the hated 'soyalinks' had been eaten. Slaughter knew he'd have to do something about it soon. He made his decision. 'All right, Corporal Young, you're in charge here.'

The volunteer flushed with pleasure, despite his weariness. 'Yessir,' he said smartly.

Sotto voce, Spiv said, 'Crap, said the Lord and a thousand arseholes bent and took the strain, for in them days the word of the Lord was law.'

Slaughter also smiled wearily. As long as his men could pull the same old hoary jokes, they were not beaten. 'I heard that, Spiv,' he said. 'Now, do you feel up to coming with me to do a recce? See what we can find in the way of shelter and grub.'

'Lead on, sir. I'm with you.' He pushed the Bren gun towards Young. 'Here you are, Corp, you're in charge now.'

Young blushed even more.

Five minutes later, as they emerged from the white dunes, the storm hit them with its full fury. Almost immediately visibility was reduced to virtually nil. The wind screamed straight in from the sea, bringing with it a solid wall of bitter rain. Within a matter of minutes the two lone men on that remote

234

beach were drenched, their uniforms cling-
ing to them, black and soaked. But despite
the discomfort, Slaughter was glad of the
pouring rain. It provided them with the
cover they needed, for now, peering through
the storm, he could just make out what
appeared to be a coastal road running in the
direction of Swinemunde and, in the gaps
between the pelting raindrops, he thought
he caught a glimpse of people and vehicles
crawling along it.

'What d'yer think, skipper?' Spiv asked as
they paused for a moment and peered at the
road.

'Dangerous, admittedly,' Slaughter gasped, wiping the raindrops off his brick-red
face. 'But where there's people, there's got
to be food – maybe even, with a bit of luck,
fuel for the skimmer. We'll just have to
chance it, Spiv. But keep your eyes skinned
for trouble.'

'Like the proverbial tinned tomato, sir,'
Spiv answered in his usual cocky fashion.
He loosened the pistol he had stuck down
his belt and then, as an afterthought, he
transferred the grenade to his trouser
pocket, saying to no one in particular, 'Just
in case.'

They went on, bodies bent against the
raging storm, the sound of voices being

carried towards them in pauses in the howling wind. To their front, on the slightly elevated coastal road, it seemed the whole of Pomerania was on the move. The road was packed with miserable civilians pushing or dragging their possessions in prams and handcarts, slung over creaking bicycles with flat tyres. Mingled with them were the retreating German infantry, trying to maintain some kind of discipline under the command of officers who marched with drawn pistols or machine pistols cocked over their arms. It was clear that the soldiers had no heart for combat any more. Here and there on each side of the road, dead soldiers hung from the telegraph poles, heads twisted to one side, tongues like strips of purple leather, with crude placards adorning their chests, proclaiming that they were 'Traitors to the Fatherland' and 'Defeatists'.

Slaughter didn't hesitate. No one was taking any notice of the two drenched men standing in the field below. The eyes of the fugitives were fixed on their front with a kind of fervent longing. It said, 'Let's get out of here before the Russians come.'

'Come on,' Slaughter urged. 'Let's get in with 'em for a while, till we find what we want.' Moments later they had vanished into that procession of despair and misery.

Two

Lofty should have known better. Rosie with her bad temper and the Russian pistol together were a bad combination, especially as the hot-blooded Scot was burdened with Nellie Dean and was in no mood to conceal her anger at the men of this world who had done such terrible things to her friend. It was not surprising then that when the two women were challenged by the short-panted Hitler Youth, she lost her temper.

'*Nix versteh*,' she snorted as the soaked kids in their wet uniform drew them out of the crowd of numb, bent-shouldered refugees who filled the coastal road. '*Nix versteh*, yer little German bastard.' Then she added, 'Awa ter ye mother's tit!'

The two boys armed with rifles, who obviously took their duties at the checkpoint very seriously, might not have understood the broad Scots, but they did understand that the red-faced woman was not taking their authority very seriously, and the youths who were prepared to die for their Führer at the drop of a hat most desperately wanted to be taken seriously. '*Raus*!' the taller of the two snapped, raindrops running down his skinny face, prodding Rosie with the muzzle of his old-fashioned rifle.

'*Raus,* yer frigging self!' Rosie retorted.

Next to her a weak and still bleeding Nellie whispered, 'Be calm, Rosie, for God's sake. We don't want any trouble.'

But Rosie was in no mood to be calm. Instinctively her hand dropped to the pistol in her pocket. Some twenty yards behind her, Lofty, who was with the German Jewess Lisa, gasped with shock. She prayed that the Scot wouldn't do anything foolish. At the very last moment Rosie took her hand away and Lofty could have fainted with relief. But Rosie and Nellie were not out of the woods yet, it seemed.

The taller of the two boys jerked his rifle towards the side of the road where a little group of soaked, miserable and frightened civilians and a couple of soldiers crouched, shoulders bent, waiting to have their papers examined. Reluctantly Rosie, holding on to a frightened Nellie's hand, went in the direction indicated and joined the others. On the road the column started to shuffle forward once more. Lofty and Lisa were forced to move with it as they were tightly jammed with the other refugees. As they passed, Rosie, stubborn and tough to the end, winked at them. Lofty cursed under her breath. What the hell was she going to do now? A few moments later they came to the top of the slight hill and vanished over the other side, leaving Rosie and Nellie to their fates.

For all her truculence, Rosie knew that she was in trouble – or she soon would be. The two German kids were taking their duty seriously, pulling people out of the seemingly endless column at regular intervals and forcing those selected to join the shivering crowd. She guessed they wouldn't be doing it unless the kids anticipated someone in authority would come along in due course and examine what they thought were suspects.

Now her mind raced as she pondered what she should do. Should she wait and take her chance of being freed again when the kids got tired of them or the Russians made an appearance on the horizon? That would be enough to frighten even these fanatical little kids in their short pants. Or should she attempt to make a run for it now? She was armed and that was something that the kids had not taken into account. She'd be able to spring a surprise upon them, and she *was* a good shot. But then she thought of poor Nellie, still shocked and bleeding from the brutal rape, who was in no way fit for swift action. Rosie bit her bottom lip. Christ, this time she had really landed herself right up the creek without the proverbial paddle. For the moment she couldn't think what she should do except hope that Lofty, big upper-class twit that she was, would break away from the column and come to their rescue. She shivered and wished that some God in a white shirt would make a miraculous appearance bringing with him a large Scotch or, better still, two large Scotches. But the kindly old gentleman in the white shirt stubbornly refused to do so. Jessie shivered again.

If Jessie was troubled and confused about what to do next, so was Lofty. Some of the other girls had already passed her and were heading with the rest of the dreary, soaked column towards the ports, heads bent like people being sent to their death, which perhaps they were. Now she and Lisa sat slumped on the roadside, unable to continue any further, too weary and soaked to be intimidated by the threats of the guards, who were now intent on putting as much space as possible between themselves and the pursuing Russians. Naturally the SS, who would bring up the rest of the column, would be different, Lofty knew that. They wouldn't hesitate. For them it would be shoot first and ask questions afterwards. But Lofty reasoned that it would be some time before the SS caught up with them – besides, she could hear the muted snap and crackle of a small arms fight over the steady drumbeat of the pouring rain. Perhaps the SS were already pinned down by the Russians. At all events, she still had time to help rescue Jessie and Nellie, she hoped.

'I think we can go back now, Lofty,' Lisa whispered close to her ear. 'There seems to be a break in the guards, and the infantry.' She indicated the soldiers, laden down like pack mules with equipment, now filing past them. 'They're too busy saving their own necks to worry about us, I think.'

Lofty nodded. 'You're right.' She rose stiffly, her soaked clothes sticking to her unpleasantly. Lean on me as if you've hurt your leg or something. If someone tries to stop us, speak to them in German. Tell 'em I'm your Polish maid or something and you're fleeing East Prussia. You're not well and I'm taking you to that barn over there to get shelter for the night. Anything that

241

gets us off the hook,' she added swiftly. Lisa nodded her understanding.

It was just then that a little car, its roof protected against attack from the air by a mattress with soaked branches of a tree attached to it, came honking its way down the column, scattering the fugitives, with mud showering to left and right. Here and there the weary infantry shouted angrily and a young officer started to unsling his Schmeisser machine pistol, as if he intended to fire at the driver. In the last minute he changed his mind and raised his hand to the rim of his wet, glistening helmet in salute. It was then that Lofty caught a glimpse of the officer seated in the back, whom the young infantry lieutenant was saluting. There was no mistaking that prim, petulant face. It was that of the camp's chief intelligence officer, *Hauptmann* Fischer, the pedantic ex-teacher. Lofty's heart sank. She could guess where he was heading: to question the people who had been detained at the cross-roads by the kids of the Hitler Youth. The next moment the car had disappeared into the pouring rain and the weary column was trundling forward through the deluge once more.

Lofty felt as if someone had opened a tap and drained every bit of courage and energy from her skinny body. She and the girls, it appeared, were going to be spared nothing. Time and time again in this last terrible week, they had felt new hope that they might escape the death sentence that had been passed on them back in France the previous year, and each time their hopes had been dashed at the last moment. Now, it seemed, it was going to be the same again. For a moment she felt like simply giving up, breaking down and sobbing. But she knew she couldn't. The others depended upon her. Besides, she had been brought up to keep on fighting; it had been a family tradition. She nudged Lisa. 'Come on, we're going back. If anyone stops us, you tell them you're the German seeking attention.'

'I understand, Lofty. But when we get there, you know, what are we going to do?'

'I don't know at the moment, Lisa. All I know is we're going to try to rescue the two of them, come what may.' Her face was determined. 'Come on, Lisa. Let's not waste any more time. Off we go...'

Slaughter had just decided he and Spiv had wasted enough time – the recce had proved a failure, the few abandoned houses they'd entered had been bare of anything edible, for the column that filled the coastal road had swept through them like a horde of locusts – when he heard the voice. There was no mistaking that accent. It was straight from Glasgow: tough and harsh, aggressive as well. It was saying, 'Dinna fash yersen, Nellie – and stop yer greeting, will ye? We'll get out of this one as well.'

Spiv, who had heard too, stopped dead in his tracks, as the soaked, miserable refugees flowed to his left and right, heading to the port like lemmings. 'Cor, ferk a duck, skipper. English – well, if yer can call *that* English.'

Slaughter, his weariness forgotten in a flash, peered through the pouring rain, eyes narrowed to slits. He could just make them out. A mixed group of German civilians, others in the striped pjyamas of German concentration camps and a handful of bedraggled soldiers who had been deprived of their weapons, huddled together in soaked misery, guarded by a gang of youths in short pants, bearing rifles that were too big for them. Slaughter guessed immediately that the group had been picked out of the endless column by the kids, who looked like Hitler Youth, and were being detained there until their identity had been cleared. But where were the women who had spoken English with such a distinct Scottish accent?

'Over there, skipper,' Spiv hissed, doing the job for him. 'Sheltering under that bit of tree at eleven o'clock. See 'em?'

Slaughter did. The two of them had found a piece of cardboard box, which they held over their heads to keep off the pelting bitter rain and which seemed to act as a mike, for it had carried their voices so far. 'Yes, see 'em,' Slaughter answered, adding swiftly, 'Do you think it could be them – the women we're after?' He was wondering aloud, but in his usual cheeky fashion Spiv answered the question for him.

'There's only one way to find out, skipper.'

'And what's that?'

'To go and find out.'

Despite the misery of the rain and the tension of the moment, Slaughter grinned and told himself that he was a lucky chap to have men like Spiv under his command. They didn't come better in the whole of the British Army than his SBS troopers. 'Are you sure you're going to be able to manage with that shoulder wound of yours, Spiv?' he asked.

'A ruddy scratch, skipper,' Spiv said contemptuously. 'I've had worse wounds shaving myself. Lead on, sir.'

'Right then, here we go.' It was then that they heard the sound of a motor in low gear approaching, its driver sounding his horn angrily as he drove against that human tide of despair and misery heading the other way, and even as they heard it before they could see it, Slaughter knew instinctively that the car signified trouble.

Three

Bogodan twisted his cap around till the peak was to the back of his cropped Slavic head and commanded, 'Up periscope!'

There was the hiss of compressed air and the gleaming metal slid upwards while he waited impatiently for what it would soon reveal. Next to him Piotr watched the crew, each man at his apparatus, tense and attentive, knowing that the enemy was all around them. They had to be on their toes.

Bogodan clapped the handles of the periscope down, bent slightly and pressed his eyes to the eyepiece. A flurry of white water and a section of grey sky came into view. It wasn't enough. But he was being careful. He didn't want to take the 'scope up to its full range yet, just in case some Fritz craft had already spotted it.

He counted off the seconds. Nothing. No boom of gunfire or throb of racing engines to indicate that he was being attacked. Behind him Piotr checked the hydrophone operators and whispered, *'Horoscho, tova-rich!'*

Bogodan took a slight breath and then eased the 'scope up higher. Immediately everything came into view. He turned up the image-amplifier. The picture became clearer. Just to make sure that he had not been spotted, Bogodan spun the 'scope round through 360 degrees. The sea was full of shipping, both civilian and naval. But most of the enemy craft were at anchor, apart from a few supply boats chugging back and forth between the grey-painted destroyers and S-boats. No one at all seemed to have noticed the telltale periscope that had appeared in their midst.

Pleased that they had penetrated to the enemy's major anchorage without being discovered, Bogodan took a more leisurely survey of the area, while the operators behind him tensed over their green-glowing instruments dials and gauges, waiting for the first sign of danger. At his side he could hear his first officer Piotr begin to breathe more heavily. He knew why. Piotr knew that every extra minute they spent close to the surface spelled increasing danger. It took only one low-flying Fritz plane to spot their silhouette beneath the still water of the anchorage and they'd be in serious trouble.

But Bogodan didn't allow himself to be hurried. A veteran of two years of submarine warfare in the narrow confines of the Black Sea, he felt confident he could outfool the Fritzes, even when there were so many of them. He guessed they were too busy with the problem of evaluating the beaten German Army and the thousands of civilians to think of an enemy submarine being so close inland.

Using the enhancer so that everything sprang into closer proximity, he surveyed the sea off Swinemunde, calculating size and distance with the aid of the circle of calibrated glass that was the periscope sight. The enemy ships came in varying sizes and it was obvious that the Germans were using anything seaworthy, including what looked like coal barges, to evacuate their people. Then he saw what he was looking for. His shoulder muscles tensed with the realization that he had found her. Behind him Piotr asked urgently, '*Sto?*'

By way of answer, Bogodan took a step backwards and offered the periscope to his second in command. 'Take a look. Verify, please.'

Eagerly Piotr turned his cap round and pushed it to the back of his curly head. For a moment he peered through the periscope before saying excitedly, 'You're right, Comrade Captain. It's her all right. No denying it. I mugged up the silhouette last night in the tables. It's the *Vaterland*.'

'Yes,' Bogodan agreed. 'And she's riding high in the water, you'll have noticed. She's not loaded yet, but by look of things she will be soon.'

Piotr frowned, as if he had suddenly thought of something unpleasant. 'But she's surrounded by escort craft, including a couple of *Moewe*-class Fritz detroyers as far as I can make out. Bit hard to get near to her,' he added with typical submariner's understatement.

'I've realized that,' Bogodan answered. 'But there is a way. It might be dangerous, though. He shrugged. 'But, comrade, that's our business. Die young and make a handsome corpse.'

Piotr looked at his old comrade. The skipper wasn't normally given to such gallows humour. He wondered why he was now, but he didn't dwell on the matter. Instead he asked, 'What do you propose?'

'We've got to frighten the escort craft off and, if possible, make the *Vaterland* move into deeper water where we will have a better chance of slipping her a tin fish.' He meant a torpedo. 'But first she must be fully laden. That's what the people in the Kremlin want. A fully laden ship of great tonnage.' He frowned and, before Piotr could ask any more questions, he rasped, 'Periscope down ... prepare to dive.'

Piotr echoed the orders. A few moments later she reached the required depth and started to move out on her diesels, the interior now buzzing with excitement as the crew understood the skipper's intentions. Only Bogodan did not share that excitement, for now, suddenly, he had realized the full implications of what he planned for the German liner, and they weren't pleasant.

Two kilometres away the harassed and frightened German authorities – for now the Russians were beginning to shell the outskirts of Swinemunde – worked all out to prepare the little fleet carrying the defeated army and panicked civilians across the Baltic. It wasn't easy. There were deserters and officials who had abandoned their posts before the advancing Russians and were prepared to offer everything and do anything to get on board the rescue ships, for they knew they'd be the last to sail for the safety of Schleswig-Holstein. Once the Russians, covered by the ever-increasing artillery barrage, attacked, that would be the end of the rescue operation. Admiral Doenitz, in charge of operations in northern Germany, would no longer be prepared to risk his ships, especially his precious naval vessels, in the dangerously narrow waters of the Baltic. Already at his headquarters at Murwik he was receiving reports of ever more Russian submarines entering the inland sea. The Russians were pouring them in, it seemed, to take advantage of the mass of transports waiting, as if on a silver platter, to be sunk.

In Swinemunde the docks and the streets leading up to the tenders waiting to take the fugitives to the ships out in the harbour were packed with weary infantrymen, some with bloody bandages around their wounded heads. They contrasted with the elegant ladies in thick furs, wearing all their jewellery, the diamonds that might pay for their escape, for the German mark was now totally worthless. There were the mistresses of the senior officers – Polish, Russian, Estonians – dumped here by their former lovers, selling their bodies if necessary to the begrimed sailors and stokers in order to obtain a passage, for they knew if the Russians caught them they would be dead. And everywhere there were the outpourings of the camps, eyes bulging from emaciated faces, dressed in their ragged striped pyjamas, dragging their feet behind them, as if their wooden clogs weighed a ton, begging for crusts of bread from the soldiers who had no bread themselves.

In vain the authorities tried to keep control of the situation, but they were overwhelmed. They set up soup kitchens for the civilians, but they were stormed almost at once by the starving infantrymen and by the time the 'chain-dogs', the military police, had restored orders by firing a volley over the rioters' heads, the great steaming carts bearing precious soup had been overturned and the cobbled street was running with thick green-pea soup.

By now soldiers were looting the houses. Not for food – there was none – but for women's dresses, for they knew that women would be the first to be allowed on the rescue ships. Others 'bought' babies from crooks and black marketeers. Mothers with babies would have top priority on the tenders going out to the bigger ships. Once through the security checks they had been ordered to throw the baby to the crook waiting on the quay, who would 'sell' the baby on again. Sometimes the deserters' aim wasn't so good and the squealing baby would fall into the water. Sometimes, other deserters who didn't have the money to purchase a baby would catch the falling child and run away with it, pursued by the angry owner.

Gradually as the day wore on, with the Russian fire growing ever more intense and Russian artillery spotters' planes circling the doomed port like predatory hawks, Swinemunde descended further and further into mass confusion and chaos. Now it would only take the appearance of the first Russians in the suburbs for the city to turn into complete panic.

Four

Hauptmann Fischer didn't hesitate. He got out of the car and, even before the taller of the two Hitler Youth boys attempted to report, he pushed him to one side imperiously and strode straight for the little group of shivering detainees. Almost immediately they saw his *Wehrmacht* uniform some of them started to complain or plead that they had been wrongfully arrested by the 'silly kids in short pants'. *Hauptmann* Fischer didn't even attempt to listen to their complaints. He shoved his way through them to where Rosie, hiding her face, attempted to support Nellie, who was on the verge of fainting once more.

'Ah, ah,' he said mockingly and gave a little bow, 'I see I am having the company of the English miladies once more.'

Rosie knew they had been rumbled. It was no use trying to bluff the ex-schoolmaster; he knew who they were all right. Her temper flared. She snapped, 'Go and shove yer

"English miladies" up yer Jerry arse! I'm a Scot.'

'Tut-tut,' Fischer said without rancour, knowing that he was in full charge of the situation. 'Such language for a lady, even if she is Scottish.'

'Kiss my arse!' Rosie remained as stubborn as ever, though she now knew she was facing sudden death.

Fischer took his time. Behind him as his bodyguard-driver covered the two women with his machine pistol, he took off his pince-nez and wiped the raindrops off the lenses carefully. 'I will not waste time,' he continued. 'Where are the others?' He clamped the glasses back on his beaky nose. 'Please not to delay. Otherwise I will have you shot. Heinz!'

The young soldier raised his machine pistol and clicked off his safety catch. He aimed the Schmeisser at Rosie.

Rosie felt her knees turn to water, but her face revealed nothing of her fear; it remained as defiant as ever.

'Well?' Fischer demanded. 'I give you to three.' Slowly, as if he were conducting an exercise with his pre-war students, he began counting.

'Nobble 'em,' Slaughter roared, hesitating no longer.

Despite his wound, Spiv needed no urging. He launched himself forward. In the very instant that Heinz raised his machine pistol to fire, Spiv caught him in the guts. He went down gasping like a deflating balloon. Spiv didn't give him a chance to recover. He smashed the elbow of his good arm into the bodyguard's face. Something splintered with a loud crack. Blood started to pour from the man's smashed nose. He went down on to his knees. Spiv didn't let up. As the man's hands went up to his shattered face, Spiv kneed him under the chin. He flew backwards and hit the wet gleaming tarmac without another sound, unconscious or dead before he hit the road.

Fischer blanched. Desperately he tried to tug his pistol out of his holster, crying meaningless words in his utter fear. Slaughter grinned. It wasn't a pleasant sight. But he knew these men who ordered death from behind a desk. He had the utmost contempt for them. He was now going to enjoy himself. He slapped Fischer left and right across the cheeks. His glasses flew off.

'*Bitte ... bitte ... nicht schlagen*,' he pleaded, weeping now with fear. '*Ich habe eine Frau und Kinder...*'

The words died on his lips as Slaughter slammed his fist into the ex-schoolmaster's stomach. He went down gasping as the two Hitler Youth kids, startled by this sudden change of events, came forward, pushing their way through the suspects, *'Was ist hier los?'* the taller of the two cried, full of himself, knowing that these people, despite being adults, were afraid of him.

Not now, they weren't. Suddenly, frighteningly, like some wild beast turning on its long-time trainer, the detainees turned on the self-important kids. 'Little swine,' they cried, 'who the hell do you think you are? Why, you bastards should be at home suckling on yer mother's tit instead of playing shitting soldiers.' In an instant the angry mob had ripped the weapons from the boys' grip. A moment later they were on the ground, screaming hysterically for mercy as the mob kicked them to death.

Slaughter wasted no more time on Fischer. He grabbed his pistol and shot him on the spot. He died without a murmur and then the two men and four women were running into the storm, heading back to the skimmer, while behind them the mob continued their murder of the deluded children.

Half an hour later, as the flames started to rise into the drenched night sky, back at the skimmer, they started to make their plans.

Soaked, starving and worn to the bone as they might be, they were suddenly filled with a new confidence. Watching them, Corporal Young, the greenhorn, was proud to belong to such a group.

They had done the impossible, something he had thought they couldn't do. They had found the women in the midst of a war-torn Germany, that was falling to pieces by the minute. It had cost the lives of the men of Number Two Skimmer, but he knew by now that you had to pay a price for everything. Now as he huddled under his groundsheets with the rest, the wind howling in from the sea, the shingle slithering back and forth noisily on the shore, he could hear the confidence and certainty in their voices as they planned what to do next: a handful of brave men and women against the might of what was left of Nazi Germany. As he listened to their bold plan, which some might have felt was absolutely crazy – impossible – he told himself that they were going to pull it off. There was no alternative. They had to.

'There's no way we can cross Germany. The whole bloody place is in a helluva mess,' Slaughter was saying. 'Our own chaps, the Yanks, the Russians, all fighting the Jerries. Hundreds of thousands of German civilians are on the move from east to west, German armies retreating or trying to move on Berlin to save the capital from the Russians.' He paused a moment for breath, for Slaughter was not used to making such long speeches. He looked at the women huddled together for warmth, sharing the contents of a tin of the disgusting soya links, which they had discovered in the skimmer. 'Besides, you ladies are not in a fit state to undertake many scores of miles marching under those conditions.'

'We could try, Captain,' Lofty said stoutly, pausing as she savoured the taste of the artificial sausage that seemed like heaven to her after the camp's thin gruel full of rotten vegetables.

'Aye, yer ken we can,' Rosie added. 'Those Jerry bastards'll have to get up early in the morning to catch Mrs Mackenzie's pretty daughter.' She glared at Slaughter.

Slaughter laughed. 'Well said. But we've got to face facts. So this is what we're going to do. The only way we can get across to the other side of the Baltic now is by boat – and the only boats going that way are Jerry.' He looked at their dirty, wet faces in the gloom. 'So that means we've got to chance the risk of discovery for perhaps some twenty-four hours or so till we reach one of those ports in Schleswig-Holstein. I know we're taking a great chance, but it's the only way.' He forced a grin. 'You might say we'll be under the protection of the German Army for a day or so.'

'But, skipper,' Spiv, always quicker off the mark than the rest of the SBS troopers, objected. 'Let's say we reach this Schles-thingabob-place. That's in the hands of the Jerries as well. We won't be safe there either, skipper.'

'It's a chance we've got to take,' Slaughter replied. 'And for all I know, our people on the Elbe and Aller rivers have already started their attack on the last German defences up there. Besides, we can assume that there's some kind of order up there, which there isn't here. Here anything could happen to us and nobody would be the wiser. Over in Schleswig-Holstein, the bigwigs will be scared shitless about doing anything for which they can be brought to trial once we've captured them.'

Lofty nodded agreement and swallowed the rest of the delightful vegetable sausage, wishing the next moment she hadn't for she would dearly have liked to savour it a little longer. 'So what kind of vessel have you decided upon, Captain?'

'A big one – the biggest,' he answered promptly. 'There are a few of them out there in the bay. I saw them earlier. Why a big one?' Slaughter answered his own question. 'Because we're least likely to be spotted among a large number of passengers of all shapes, sizes, uniform, civvies and the like. Undoubtedly there'll be foreigners among them, too, people who worked for the Germans, members of those foreign auxiliaries that the Jerries used in the *Wehrmacht* on the Russian front and the like. If we keep our heads down and our mouths shut,' Slaughter looked pointedly at Spiv, 'with a bit of luck, we'll pull it off...'

'As the actress said to the bishop,' Spiv interjected smartly and Slaughter gave a helpless little laugh. 'See what I mean, ladies.'

But Spiv's intervention had broken the tension. Now, as the storm continued to rage, churning the sea to a white fury, they made their plans until Slaughter ordered that they must now all sleep for a couple of hours before they set off along the coast. But not even Young, the teenager, who could normally fall asleep at the bat of an eyelid, could rest. They were too preoccupied with what was soon to come, each one of them wrapped up in a cocoon of his or her thoughts.

In the end Slaughter gave up. He sat up

and pushed aside the dripping branches that had offered him some protection against the rain and said huskily, 'It's no use. I don't think any of us can sleep. I think we might as well get started.' Then he pulled a little surprise upon his soaked men and their new female guests. 'You chaps have my permission to break into your emergency rations and share them with the ladies.'

'Stone the crows!' Spiv cried. 'I'd forgotten about that. Well, I'll go to our house.' He and the others wasted no time. It was at least twelve hours since they had eaten the last of the compo rations. They broke the seal of the brass tins in their right breast pockets and took out the bitter dark chocolate. Suddenly, as greedy as they were for the rationed chocolate, they played the perfect gentlemen now. 'No, miss, you have the bigger slab ... Would you like a little more, miss? They say it's full of vitamins.' Slaughter could have laughed at them, but he didn't. At that moment he felt like crying. What men! So they set off into the wild night, sucking the bitter Rowntrees chocolate.

The night was ideal for their purpose. Despite the storm, they made good progress: five kayaks tied together with the commando toggle ropes, towing the light skimmer that held the women. Despite the heavy weight, they kept perfect time, paddling at a steady, even pace. In the first kayak, Young was their lookout, swinging his head from side to side as he paddled, routinely scanning the dark horizon for the first sign of danger.

But there was none. It was as if they were alone in the world, a handful of puny mortals set in this vast limitless sea, with a storm raging, intent on wiping them off the face of the miserable universe. But they were not to die *yet*, and as the dawn broke once again and the storm diminished to reveal a great liner to their front, slaughter announced confidently, 'That's her ... That's the ship we want.'

From mouth to mouth they passed the words back to the women on the skimmer, from whence someone cried, 'What's her name?'

Slaughter focused his glasses and after a moment cried back, 'Wouldn't you know it ... typical German ... She's called the *Vaterland*.'

Five

Now the sirens started to wail the 'all clear' at last. To the west the majestic silver giants, which had brought death and destruction from so far, started to depart for their bases in England and France. Behind them the naval flak continued firing purposelessly, peppering the morning sky with the cherry-red of exploding shells. Slowly the Flying Fortresses closed ranks, filling in the gaps where comrades had been shot out of the sky, their gunners ready in the new boxes to meet the German fighters further west.

'Bloody Brylcreem boys,' Spiv spat. 'Back off home to their frigging bacon and frigging eggs, no doubt.' But he said the words without rancour. The dawn air raid on Swinemunde had provided them with the cover they had needed. Hurriedly they had pushed the kayaks out to sea and buried the skimmer beneath the water and, together with the women, they had stolen into the port unseen, the American bombs exploding all around them. And they had been lucky, too.

One of the US bombs had hit what appeared to be a naval store not far from the quayside. By the garish light of the incendiaries they could see the quartermaster staff hanging from the skeletal trees in bloody pieces, dripping with blood like some human passion fruits. The women had turned away from the gruesome sight, sickened and appalled.

Not Slaughter. He had seen his chance to get some food, and anything else that was going, while the port authorities were fully engaged trying to douse the fires that were springing up everywhere. 'Come on,' he had commanded, shouting above the shrill whine and harsh crunch of the exploding bombs. 'Follow me ... at the double ... There's no time to be lost.'

The women hesitated. But not the SBS troopers. They were too hungry and chilled by the storm to be squeamish. They pushed by the hunks of human flesh hanging from the trees, dodging the blood dripping from them, and pressed their way through the rubble into the smoking store.

Inside, the horror of the bombed quayside was forgotten. 'Hell's bells,' Spiv cried and slapped his good hand to his forehead in wonder. 'I'm in frigging heaven! Pinch me, somebody.'

But the others were too overcome by what they could see by the lurid, flickering light of the flames outside. There was food the like of which the SOE women had not seen for many months. Rows of great ham shanks, lines of salami and rings of sausage hung from the racks everywhere. Shelves bulged with tins of meat. Salted butter in barrels lay above line after line of expensive wines stolen and looted from what had once been the Nazi Empire. So they stood in awe, the offer to pinch Spiv unheeded, until Slaughter snapped, 'Look lively. Let's get as much of this stuff as we can and find somewhere to cook it ... And don't forget those eggs.'

The others knew what he meant. After years of rationing in Britain, where the motto had been 'one egg, per person, per week, *per-haps*', all of them craved eggs. Even Young, the greenhorn, was beginning to salivate at the thought of a couple of fried eggs, a delicacy he had not yet experienced in his nineteen years on earth.

Now as the bombers departed and the port came to frantic life again, with refugees torn between looting and reaching the quays to stand in line for ships to take them away from this horror, Slaughter and his replete charges planned their own rescue attempt, knowing that now, with their pockets bulging with looted cigarettes, they had the necessary bribes to see them through most of the anticipated checks.

Corporal Young, wiping the yellow of an egg from his mouth, said thickly, 'There seems to be a line of those military police-men close to the tenders, sir. They'll be tough to get through, I think, sir.'

Slaughter turned away from the shattered window that overlooked the quayside and addressed the others, men and women, slumped on the floor, breathing hard and holding their distended stomachs as if they were in acute pain. 'We're not going to try to get through the MP cordon. I don't think those chaindogs, as the Jerries call 'em, will be bribable.'

'What do we do then, Captain Slaughter?' Lofty asked, still chewing on the end of a spicy Italian salami, extracting every last bit of nourishing juice from it like a greedy baby sucking its mother's breast.

'We tackle the sailors who man the tenders taking the refugees out to the big ships in the bay.'

'But how we gonna do that, skipper?' Spiv enquired. 'To get to them we've got to get through the MPs.'

'No, we haven't, Spiv. You know these wooden quays. They're hollow beneath. They're wooden platforms supported on concrete or steel pylons for the most part, to allow the sea in and out without damaging the structure. We're going to go *underneath* the quay, not *over* it.'

Lofty looked impressed. 'Smart thinking, Captain.'

Slaughter allowed himself a careful, wintry smile. 'Thank you. But it's not altogether that brilliant. It could be risky, too. We're probably not the first to think of the same idea and the authorities might already have made provision to stop anyone using that method of getting to the ship's tenders. At all events we've got to be on our toes.'

His warning didn't seem to depress his listeners. The food had worked wonders and Lisa said to Young, speaking for all the women really, 'You men have been the best thing we've encountered in these many months. I think we have a good chance now, thanks to you.' She touched his arm tenderly and Young felt himself blushing furiously. Muttering something that he felt was probably silly, he added, 'Thank you. Now I must go.'

Five minutes later, divided into two groups, one led by Slaughter, the other by

Young, they made their way through the still-burning streets of the dock area, heading for the quayside. As a burning roof opposite slithered to the ground, making them jump with surprise, they turned the corner and saw the full horror of the American air raid. There were dead people everywhere, spread out in unnatural postures. The living looked little better. Some were nearly naked, their upper bodies smeared with soot and blood. A couple of blind men were being led by another holding on to a broom pole. Wounded were being pushed by their weeping relatives in prams or barrows like grotesque overgrown scarlet babies. A woman, crying hysterically, sat on the kerb trying to suckle a dead body.

Slaughter frowned and tried not to let himself be affected by the horror all around him. It was part and parcel of total war, he told himself. He'd seen it all before. He hoped that this would be the last time he'd ever see it.

He turned a corner and nearly stepped on a woman, her clothes stripped from her body by the blast, her legs open to reveal her most intimate parts: an obscene invitation even in death.

Now more and more civilians were thronging the street ahead, aiming for the tenders guarded by the circle of grim-faced, helmeted German military policemen, the silver gorget of their calling around their necks, their carbines at the ready. The civilians streamed in from all sides, children screaming with pain, hopping along on their pathetic sticks of wounded legs like little human rabbits. Women, eyes bulging from their heads, faces ashen under newly white hair, screamed silently. Mad women. Old men were coughing and choking with smoke as if in their death throes. Wounded servicemen lay in their striped blue pyjamas, minus legs, arms, eyes. Carts bore the dead, some shrunken to the size of pygmies by the scorching heat of the inferno; others without heads, legs, everything. Horror upon horror.

Slaughter was not a fanciful man. But as he and the others advanced on the tenders, the doleful procession of woe seemed to him like some medieval woodcut of the victims of the Black Death, trying to escape from a skeletal Grim Reaper from whom there was no escape. Behind him, Corporal Young breathed, 'Thus ends the One Thousand Year Reich.'*

* Name given to Hitler's Third Reich, which lasted exactly twelve years.

'Gawd almighty,' Spiv breathed in mock awe further down the file. 'Ain't you the clever one, Corp, knowing all that stuff.'

As always Young flushed and Lisa whispered, 'Take no notice of him. He's jealous.' Young's flush deepened even more. This was the first time that a woman had ever taken any real interest in him. Despite everything he felt a sudden warm glow of happiness.

Somehow they got through that terrible procession, which was now being halted by the chaindogs checking for passes and trying to weed out the deserters, several of whom were clad in women's dresses with shawls bound round their heads to conceal their cropped heads. Already behind the wrecked sheds they could hear the rattle of tommy guns. They had already begun to shoot the deserters without trial. Slaughter frowned. If anything went wrong now, he told himself grimly, and they fell into the hands of the helmeted military policemen, they could expect no mercy. Man or woman, they would be shot out of hand. Slaughter determined, come what may, that they wouldn't be caught.

It was about then that he spotted the bomb hole in the wooden surface of the quayside. It looked as if a bomb had splintered the wood, gone through it and dropped to the dirty, oil-scummed water below without exploding. It wasn't a big hole, but it was big enough for them, and it was partially concealed by the bodies, already stiffening in the dawn cold, piled up to one side like a collection of logs. Hastily he indicated that they should stay where they were. Alone he darted forward to inspect the hole, crouching low behind the bodies so that the chaindogs busy to his front next to the tenders couldn't see him.

He peered down to the water below, lapping idly about the concrete piles.

It seemed all right to him. Bending down, he craned his head forward and caught a glimpse of one of the tenders waiting to take the fugitives to the big ships, with a lone sailor smoking fitfully at the bow. He peered harder and there it was – the name of the ship, the one he had already selected. *Vaterland*.

Slaughter waited no longer. He stuck two fingers into his mouth and, like some backstreet urchin, whistled shrilly the signal to the others. Moments later they were climbing down into the holes, the SBS troopers supporting the women, weakened by months of imprisonment on starvation rations, as best they could.

Over to the east of the city the sirens started to shrill their warning once more. Another air attack and, to judge by the direction it was coming from, Slaughter guessed that this time the attackers would be Russian. That didn't worry Slaughter. The air raid would provide the cover they needed. Now it all depended on whether the sailors on the tender could be bribed. If they couldn't – Slaughter's jaw hardened and he gripped the butt of his pistol concealed beneath his waistband – there were other means to make the Jerries agree. Moments later he was scaling down the beams after the others, as if he couldn't get to the tender quickly enough. The final stage of their escape had commenced.

Six

Bogodan took one last quick look through the periscope and barked sharply, 'Down tube!'

Smoothly the periscope slid down into the green-glowing fetid atmosphere of the Soviet submarine. There were the young crew, all now bearded save for Amoy, the Tartar who never grew hair.

Bogodan, mindful of what he had just seen on the surface, took his time, mulling over his tactics. Finally after Piotr had cleared his throat significantly twice, he said, 'Comrades, we shall fire one torpedo using the tube. The fish had to sit perfectly to clear the way for the two torpedoes we will fire blind. The fish are a revolutionary weapon. They can't miss. Once we've fired 'em, they'll do the job without us, and we'll do a bunk for safety.' Bogodan looked around the circle of pallid, bearded faces, knowing that his last words had cheered them up no end. All of them knew what to expect after they'd

275

fired number one tube. All hell would be let loose and they wanted to be as far away as possible from that particular fiendish hell. '*Horoscho*,' he said to end his little speech. 'To your duty stations.' He nodded for Piotr to come closer. He lowered his voice, so that the crew couldn't hear. 'It's going to be hairy, Piotr. But it's got to be done if we're gonna stick one up the *Vaterland*'s fat Fritz arse.'

'I understand, skipper,' the other officer replied. He knew the plan already. They'd fire at one of the *Vaterland*'s escort vessels that surrounded the great liner. With luck they'd hit and start her sinking with that first tin fish. That would raise the alarm and they planned – and hoped – the Fritzes would scatter and come looking for them, believing that their attacker would already be making a run for it. Then in the same position they'd give the *Vaterland* the benefit of a clear torpedo run with the two other fish.

'It's a simple plan,' Bogodan said, apparently reading his second in command's mind. 'But often these simple plans work best.'

'And if the Fritz asdic locks on to us straight away, while we're preparing to fire from the same position?'

276

Bogodan shrugged. 'We'll make handsome corpses, Piotr. Let's get on with it.'

Five minutes later, the submarine crept ever closer to its target at slow speed. Now all machines were kept at their lowest sound level and when the crewmen had to speak, they did so in whispers. It was as if they half-expected the enemy to be listening to them, ear pressed to the other hull.

Now they were in shooting range and in a dangerous position. The nearest enemy craft would be less than a kilometre away. The crewmen could feel the danger as something tangible, the tension heightened by the eerie silence of the submarine. Even Bogodan, the veteran, could feel a cold finger of fear trace its way down the small of his back. He shuddered involuntarily and forced himself to concentrate on the task at hand. 'Slow ahead both,' he whispered. The hum of the electric motors grew even fainter. He licked his lips and then commanded, 'Up periscope.'

There was the usual hiss of compressed air as the gleaming silver tube shot by him and surfaced. Swiftly he seized the instrument and, as the sight broke the water, he took another glance at his target. It was one of the smaller *Moewe* class destroyers. He knew from the tables that the class was very fast, but lightly armoured. With a bit of luck she'd sink straight off and that would set the cat among the pigeons. He knew the Fritzes; they'd be eager for revenge and be swarming out to find the Russian sub that had dared to sink one of their newest destroyers.

Swiftly he gave his instructions. Behind the petty officers readied their torpedoes. In the green eerie light of the interior of the hull, their strained faces dripped with sweat. All of them knew that what happened in the next few seconds might well end in sudden death for them. But Bogodan had no time to concern himself with such matters. He wasted no more time. Raising his voice automatically, he cried, *'Fire ... Fire ... Fire One!'*

The boat shuddered. A faint splash. The two-ton torpedo had hit the water. He flashed a look at the trim meter. It was all right. Hastily he ordered, 'Hard left rudder ... steer two fifty.' Their course changed immediately as the electric motors started humming loudly once again. Just behind him, Piotr started to count off the seconds with his stopwatch while Bogodan pressed his eye to the periscope.

As the scientists of the Leningrad Naval Institute had promised, there were no tell-tale bubbles to give away the course of the torpedo. Bogodan waited. Behind him Piotr counted off the seconds, the sweat greasing his pale face like Vaseline. Bogodan found himself gripping the controls of the periscope, as if he were trying to crush the steel handles.

A sudden shudder. A muffled roar. The submarine lurched as if a gigantic fist had slammed into her hull. Piotr grabbed hold of a stanchion. His face was abruptly wreathed in a smile. He knew what had happened. They had hit something with their torpedo.

Frantically Bogodan adjusted the periscope sight. He swung the tube round. The green mist of the leaping waves fell back. 'We've done it!' he yelled wildly as the sinking destroyer slid into the bright gleaming circle of the calibrated glass. The torpedo had struck the *Moewe* class amidships. Now she was breaking in half, thick smoke pouring from her engine room, her bow already awash, while panic-stricken sailors were already beginning to throw themselves into the icy Baltic. Behind the crew began to cheer. They knew there would be vodka soon for them on account of this victory.

Piotr waited expectantly for Bogodan's verdict as he peered through the periscope. 'We got her,' the former announced, trying to keep calm. 'She's sinking rapidly.'

'The others?' Piotr snapped.

'They're dispersing. A couple already seem to be getting up steam.' He pressed his eye closer to the scope. Already the first confusion of the surprise sinking had passed. Tenders were hurrying out to the sinking destroyer. They were going to rescue the men in the water, flailing wildly and trying to keep afloat. Red signal flares were hissing into the sky. Aldis lamps were clicking on and off between the naval vessels. It wouldn't be long before they were hurrying out of anchorage to look for his submarine. On the deck of what looked like a troopship, gunners were pelting for the forward cannon. Bogodan knew they hadn't the faintest idea where his craft was, but they'd pepper the area with shells as some kind of crazy defensive measure. He smiled grimly at the thought and then for his last few remaining minutes he concentrated on the huge liner that the destroyers were there to protect.

She was some two kilometres away and still taking passengers on board. He could see the tiny figures scrambling up her sides, some of them, perhaps soldiers, using nets to do so. A lazy wisp of smoke curled from her funnels. She'd obviously got up steam, but she wasn't ready to sail just yet; her anchor chains had not been raised. He smiled grimly. When she did sail, he'd ensure that she wouldn't get far. Then he remembered that the *Vaterland* might well contain fellow Russians, prisoners of the Germans, and his smile vanished.

'*Horoscho*,' he ordered. 'Take her down...' He addressed Piotr. 'Comrade Lieutenant, instruct the quartermaster to break out one hundred grams of vodka per man.'

The crew cheered, but Bogodan didn't share their happiness at the victory. His mind was too full of what was to come. Instead he said, 'Take her to one hundred and fifty metres...' Without another word, he pushed his way through the smiling, happy crew and made his way to his tiny cabin. He pulled the curtain, a sign that he didn't want to be disturbed. Silently he sat on his bunk, alone with his thoughts. They weren't pleasant...

'*Shit!*' Slaughter exclaimed as the sinking destroyer was racked by another series of explosions. He felt the blast slap his face like a blow from a fist and closed his eyes for an instant. All around him the sorely tried women refugees started to shriek and scream, while the men, many of them prisoners, lowered their heads as if they couldn't bear to watch the dying ship any longer; they'd had enough misery.

'What do you make of it?' the tall, angular female prisoner asked in her upper-class accent. 'It can't be one of our submarines, here in the Baltic, can it, Captain Slaughter?'

Slaughter hissed, 'Lower your voice, please, Lofty. We don't want them to hear us speaking English.' He pushed away from the packed railing underneath one of the *Vaterland*'s lifeboats, which he noted automatically had been holed badly by the shrapnel that had peppered her length. 'No,' he answered. 'Got to be Russian.'

'But they're our allies,' Lofty protested.

'Supposed to be,' he retorted. 'Besides, they don't know we're on board, do they?'

'But there are plenty of their own Russian people aboard. Look over there. There's a whole bunch of them still in Russian uniform.' She indicated a group of skeletal prisoners in ragged uniforms, their feet bound in rags, but wearing the fur hats of the Red Army.

Slaughter shrugged. 'We can assume the sub commander either didn't know that or didn't care in the first place.' He lapsed into silence while the big Englishwoman, who was all skin and bone, pondered the matter.

It had been easy to get aboard. The sailors manning the tender had been only too eager to do a deal. 'For cigarettes we'll take you to heaven and back, *Fraulein*,' they had gushed to Lisa, who had worked out the transfer with the aid of two cartons of cigarettes taken from the bombed quartermaster's store.

Despite the angry shouts of the chaindogs on the jetty above and the cries of those up there waiting with their pathetic bundles, the sailors had pushed off immediately. Ten minutes later they had been struggling up the ladder, again helped by those precious cigarettes, the only currency that an almost defeated Nazi Germany recognized. Almost immediately Slaughter had ordered the group to disperse, but to keep within sight and hailing distance of each other as more and more refugees were crammed into the ship. Now he was alone with Lofty while Lisa was within sight, guarded by a smitten Corporal Young. If he needed her, Lisa was at hand to speak German.

'What will happen next, Captain?' Lofty broke his brooding silence.

Slaughter hesitated, pushing the worst option to the back of his mind. 'Well, the best thing for us is if those destroyers now making steam and the other escort craft sink that Russian sub before it can signal its mates that there's a big fat juicy target like the *Vaterland* here, ready and waiting to be picked off. The next best thing is the skipper of this ship sets sail immediately, surrounding himself with all the escorts he can...' Slaughter broke off abruptly as the flashing white lights of the signallers sending messages back and forth between the escort vessels stopped and the first of the smaller craft started to leave the anchorage.

Lofty saw the look on Slaughter's face and asked urgently, 'What does that mean, Captain?'

Slaughter pursed his lips grimly. 'I'm afraid, Lofty, that means that the escorts are going to chase that bloody Russki sub. If all of 'em go, we're going to be on our lonesome. We'll have to get it across to the others. Prepare for the worst and not to hang about when the worst happens. He forced a tight smile. 'Which, probably, it won't.'

Lofty looked at the SBS officer squarely and knew that he expected the worst. Ten minutes later the anchors began to rattle and slowly, very slowly, the great liner, packed with its cargo of human misery, began to move into the bay.

★　★　★

'*Alarm!*' the man on watch yelled frantically. At their little metal desks, the operators whirled their handles and pressed their hands tighter to their earphones, faces taut in the eerie red light of the interior of the submarine.

Bogodan hit the panic button. The sirens shrilled. The off-duty watch came running from their bunks, doing up their flies, pulling on whatever equipment they needed. Suddenly, startlingly, everything was controlled chaos.

Bogodan, face grim, knew that they were now about to pay for their easy victory. But he was the veteran. He'd been through all this many times before. All the same, he knew, too, that you never got used to it.

The first pattern of depth charges hit the water. At their machines the operators waited for the noise of their attackers' screws growing louder. But they didn't. Their attackers hadn't really located the Russian submarine. A moment later the series of depth charges exploded. The sub reeled from side to side as if punched by a savage fist. Here and there a glass dial shattered under the impact. Rivets burst and flew through the air like bullets. Water started to trickle in through the buckled plates. Immediately the fitters and shipwrights went to work, plugging the holes and sealing the plates, their wooden mallets covered with thick cloth so that they didn't make too much noise. For above them, on the surface, other tense operators would be listening at their instruments trying to get a 'fix' on their enemy lurking beneath the sea.

Bogodan reacted at once. 'Stop engines,' he hissed. 'Silent running.'

The engines ceased in an instant. The submarine glided on noiselessly. The riggers ceased their work, mallets poised in mid-air, as if they had been frozen there for all eternity. Suddenly all movement ceased in the red-lit interior of the sub. The crew at their posts were motionless, hardly seeming to breathe, each man wrapped in a cocoon of his own thoughts. At the scope, which dominated the little control centre, Bogodan tensed. He was waiting for the inevitable as the sound of the enemy ship's crews came close again. Then there was that frightening ping-ping of the asdic as the German operator up above searched for the Russian submarine. Bogodan – all of them – heard that damned sound as it ran the length of the hull. If the unknown German above recognized the strength of the signal and reported it to his skipper they could expect another pattern of depth charges.

But this time they would be more effective.

The tension grew.

The seconds passed with leaden feet as the frightening ping-ping sound continued and then suddenly the noise of the hunter ship's screws died away and Piotr, as pale and tense as his captain, let out a great sigh of relief. Someone farted and the crew laughed quietly. The tension had been broken. The German operator had missed them.

Bogodan said, 'I think that the Fritzes must have been—' But his words died on his lips as the first exploding depth charge struck the sub amidships, sending her reeling to one side violently. The lights went out. Glass splintered. Plates buckled and water started to rush in. At Bogodan's side, Piotr, the fervent communist, crossed himself like some old peasant *babushka* and started to pray.

On the quarterdeck, the captain of the *Vaterland* had ordered the ship's band to commence playing. Now the elderly bandsmen, dressed in some sort of fantasy uniform, were seated on the little stools playing patriotic marches under the direction of a fierce-looking petty officer, who sported a large moustache in the style of the old Kaiser. The captain of the *Vaterland* obviously wanted to ease the tension on the packed deck. It could well have been one of those pre-war 'Strength Through Joy' cruises in the Baltic, save for one thing. On a deck above the quarterdeck, the ship's captain had posted two machine guns manned by a handful of helmeted SS guards. If the band failed to calm the passengers and there was a panic, the gunners would open up.

'German thoroughness,' Slaughter commented as the band launched into the traditional old Swabian song of departure: *'Muss i ... muss id denn'*. 'Carrots and the stick if necessary.'

Lofty pulled a face. 'Don't talk to me of German thoroughness. I've bloody had enough of it. Give me decent old British muddling through any day.'

Slaughter knew what she meant. For an instant the tall upper-class Englishwoman, normally fully in control of herself, looked bitter and angry. He could understand why. She had suffered more than a woman should at the hands of the enemy. For his part, he couldn't hate the Germans; he had long got over that phase. He was a soldier. It was his duty to fight – and kill – the Germans. But he did so dispassionately. Hate only confused a soldier in battle, made him

288

commit mistakes – and mistakes cost lives.

He said, 'Let's get back to the railing, Lofty. The crowd seems to be sticking here listening to the brass band. There's room over there now.'

She nodded. 'Good idea, Captain. But what are we to do if the *Vaterland* is attacked? The sea'll be icy and...' She shrugged eloquently, as if she didn't need to say anymore – and she didn't. Slaughter understood perfectly.

'We nobble one of the smaller lifeboats. There'll be outright panic if we are attacked. It'll be everyone for himself. We'll have to look after our own. All right?'

'Yes, all right.'

Together they pushed their way through the throng. Behind them the petty officer with the fearsome moustache raised his baton again, stamped his foot and launched his brass band into the 'Blue Danube'. Rosie, standing close by with a still-shocked Nellie Dean, growled, 'What does he expect 'em to do? Dance the frigging waltz?'

Slowly the great ship started to edge its way forward, the band playing and in the bay the little escorts circling madly, dropping their depth charges as they did so. Behind it trailed the sad strains of the Viennese waltz...

Seven

The depth charging had continued far too long. Biting, acrid fumes had begun to escape from the electric batteries. The crew choked. Here and there their eyes bulged from their sockets like the crazy gaze of the demented. Bogodan knew his younger crewmen wouldn't be able to stand the strain much longer. The constant explosions that rocked the boat and caused ever more damage to the sub's hull were becoming too much for them. Even Piotr was praying openly now, crossing himself over and over again like some sanctimonious pope.

Bogodan had ordered that those who needed them should use the potash masks, which would stop the choking feeling caused by the lack of air inside the littered hull. But those masks only had a limited life. What then?

As the screws of another attacker disappeared into the distance, Bogodan made a decision. 'Comrade Lieutenant,' he ordered

Piotr, 'we'll take her up fifty metres ... We'll take the chance.'

Piotr stopped his fervent praying. He nodded his agreement, face crimson with the lack of oxygen, his lips a bright blue. He rose slowly and then, as Bogodan watched and listened intently, he began to take the boat up in easy stages. To Bogodan it seemed that the noise of the depth charging was further away now. But he wasn't merely grabbing at straws, false hopes. He knew the Fritzes were skilled seamen, who knew their job as well as he did. They might be trying to tempt him into a trap. What had his old chief in the Black Sea said? 'The Russian has a heavy voice, but a soft hand. The Fritz, however, has a soft voice and a *very heavy hand*.'

Metre by metre the softly humming electric motors took them upwards. Finally Piotr, gasping for breath, choked, eyeing the submarine's trim. 'We ... can ... use the scope now, Comrade.'

'Up periscope,' Bogodan commanded, trying for the sake of the crew to sound keen and purposeful. He bent to take hold of the scope and felt his ears pop. Bogodan knew immediately what had happened. A vacuum had occurred in the tube. *'Quick!'* he ordered. 'Take her down.' The crew, who had taken off the potash masks in anticipation of the fresh air that should be flooding the boat, now started to gasp once more, eyes looking as if they might well pop out of their heads at any moment. Breathing became almost impossible. Men ripped at their collars, tearing at their singlets in the hope of obtaining more air.

Bogodan felt as if he might faint. There was a noisy buzzing in his ears. Stars exploded in front of his eyes. He was choking to death. With the last of his strength he kicked the scope. Something clicked. Hastily he thrust the scope upwards once more. There was no longer a jam. The air mast was functioning. Swiftly, hardly able to get the words out, he ordered the worst cases to lie on the casing beneath the exit to the air mast in order to snatch some fresh air and then move on to let the next one catch a breath.

Now he threw caution to the wind. 'Take her up, Piotr,' he cried. 'For God's sake, take her up!'

His second in command didn't object. He knew the crew were dying in front of his eyes. Some, who couldn't manage to crawl to the faint trickle of clean air, had already passed out. He took the submarine up.

Suddenly there was an obscene pop, like a

giant breaking wind. In an instant, clear air was flooding the boat. Holding on to the tube, Bogodan, his eardrums threatening to explode under the changed pressure, knew he had won. He swallowed hard. The pain vanished. He'd equalized the pressure. Now he peered through the scope. The destroyers and escort craft were vanishing seawards. They had given up the depth-charging, feeling perhaps that the Russian submarine had sailed into the bay and escaped. Wiping the sweat off his forehead with the back of his hand, Bogodan gave a weary smile. The way was clear now. He had been saved for the mission that Stalin had himself ordained. The time had come to sink the *Vaterland*...

By now the band had become weary of playing, and no one was offering the bandsmen free beer as they had done in the days of the 'Strength Through Joy' cruises. Indeed there was hardly enough water on board the great liner to give everyone a drink. Not that that worried the ship's officers. As long as there was something to drink and eat for themselves and their protective guard of middle-aged SS men who were manning the machine guns, that sufficed. In twelve hours or so they'd be off

Cuxhaven. Till then the thousands crowding the darkening deck would have to wait. After all, they were lucky to be escaping the Ivans. They could manage without food and water.

But not everyone on the *Vaterland* was prepared to accept the ship's officers' decision. Spiv was one such individual. The ex-London barrowboy wasn't about to go hungry, nor see his comrades do so.

Now he worked his way down the corridor, following the pleasant smell of cooking with his big nose, heading for the officers' galley. As he always maintained to his fellow SBS troopers, 'Officers and gents ain't like you and me, mates, they get better grub,' and now he was sure that he had been right. Indeed, his sensitive nose was telling the little cockney that the officers of the *Vaterland* were soon going to enjoy what he called 'a slap-up, knife-and-fork dinner'. Christ, they might even be getting chicken, which common folk ate only once a year, at Christmas – if they were lucky. That delightful vision encouraged him to continue his dangerous expedition into the unknown. He patted his right trouser pocket, where he had placed his revolver. If the hashslingers were cooking chicken down there, he was going to have his share one way or another.

While Spiv crept deeper into the bowels of the former liner, Corporal Young, as red and embarrassed as ever, talked to the German-Jewish girl, Lisa, entranced by that delightful foreign accent of hers. Despite her hunger and fatigue, she was a charming companion, who didn't seem as silly and flippant as the handful of English girls he had dared to speak to during his period as a recruit. Indeed, he could hardly believe she had once been a kind of a spy, a radio operator risking her life way behind enemy lines. His only fear, as he listened to her, was that she would not think him worthy of her. After all, she came from a rich family who had once owned a large department store in Leipzig. His father worked for the council and, although he had won a scholarship to the local grammar school, his parents had been unable to afford it.

But she did not seem to notice the difference in their social status. Perhaps, he reasoned, it was because of their present dangerous situation, where they needed each other. What would her attitude be once they got back to Britain – *if* they ever did get back? Would she change? He hoped not. For already he was half in love with her and making plans for the future.

Lofty was making plans, too. The war had

to be over soon and Daddy, the retired major-general, wouldn't object if she decided to resign her commission. He'd understand; she had done her bit. She'd leave London and would live on the estate. Everyone in town would tell her she'd be bored stiff with the usual round of hunting and shooting and entertaining doddery old relatives to tea. That didn't matter. She was prepared to be bored; she had had enough danger and excitement to last her for the rest of her life.

Indeed, among all the escapees, only Slaughter was *not* making plans. They were not out of danger yet; he knew that better than any of them. Besides, he was a regular. He'd go where the Army sent him and, the way the world looked at the moment, he guessed there would be other wars to be fought in the near future – lots of them. His kind would be needed until he was pensioned off or the inevitable happened and someone put a bullet through his head. Then he wouldn't have to worry how he might live off half-pay in some cheap provincial backwater. For, despite his war record, he knew the Army and his superiors. They didn't like irregulars, who joined the strange units like the Special Boat Service, especially ones like Captain Slaughter who showed little respect for superior rank and didn't know when to hold his tongue.

He looked at the mob all around him, the various races, dressed in rags and dirty uniforms, their weary and emaciated faces, animated by nothing but self-preservation, and wondered if the human race was really worth doing anything about. There was good and evil on both sides of the line. Were these the good people who were worth fighting for? He shrugged and told himself he didn't know. Not that it mattered. He had taken the King's shilling and sworn to fight for him and he assumed the King and his ministers were right and worthy of taking the side of the good. He smiled a little. What did it matter? What did anything matter, save looking after his own chaps and these poor women who had been through so much? He guessed that was as good a cause as any...

A mile or so away, Bogodan gave his orders. 'Stand by engine room,' he called to Igor. Behind him Piotr repeated the order, as Bogodan peered through the scope. It was getting dark but the blood-red ball of the spring sun poised on the horizon outlined the great stark black outline of the *Vaterland* perfectly. Carefully he swung the scope round. The escort vessels, which he had lured away from their charge by sinking the *Moewe* class destroyer, had still not returned. They were further out in the Baltic searching for the elusive Russian sub. Now the liner was protected solely by some kind of armed trawler and another smaller escort.

'*Horoscho*?' he called to Piotr.

'*Horoscho* – good,' his second in command repeated with a little smile, the ordeal of that day already forgotten. For he knew, just as Bogodan did, that the *Vaterland* didn't really stand a chance of surviving. Naturally all hell would be let loose afterwards, but with a bit of luck they would be able to make it back to the nearest Red Fleet base at Konigsberg before the Fritzes caught up with him. Then it would be vodka and girls and he'd be a 'Hero of the Soviet Union', too.

Bogodan had other things on his mind than women and decorations for the moment. As they continued to sail closer to the *Vaterland* at periscope depth, he considered his attack tactics. He had no fears that he wouldn't be able to sink the *Vaterland*. His worry was how long she'd take to sink and if in that time her radio operators would be in a position to send off signals to

298

their nearest land air force bases. In the shallow waters of the Baltic, aircraft could easily spot a submarine, even when the sub was submerged. Naturally it would be completely dark by the time the Fritz planes started to look for the sub. All the same, they would be using powerful searchlights to help them in their hunt. No, he had to do the job swiftly and efficiently, ensuring that any aerial search could be confused and delayed while he made his escape. For a moment he pursed his lips and stared at the great ship ploughing steadily through the water, heading westwards to what was left of Nazi-held Germany. Although it had to be bitterly cold as the sun vanished, the decks of the *Vaterland* were packed tight with people. There had to be thousands of them, huddled together, perhaps for warmth, guarded, as far as he could make out, by a line of uniformed machine-gunners on an upper deck.

He stroked his unshaven chin as he took it all in. It meant, he reasoned, that the people on deck might well be prisoners, perhaps even Soviet citizens kidnapped as cheap labour by the Fritzes, or ex-Red Army starved into joining the German Army as auxiliaries. He cursed under his breath as he made his decision, knowing that it was a cruel – even inhumane – thing that he was going to have to do in order to ensure the safety of his sub and its crew. But there was no other way. 'Down scope,' he ordered tonelessly.

Piotr asked hopefully, 'Have we an attack plan, Comrade Captain?'

Bogodan didn't answer. Instead he said, 'Alert the deck gunners. I want them at the gun forrard as soon as I give the order.' Then as afterthought he added, 'Comrade Lieutenant, see that I am brought a vodka now. I need it.'

Puzzled, his smile vanished abruptly, Piotr said that he would.

Eight

Spiv's heart beat faster as he crouched there behind the door of the huge galley. In front of him, on the immaculate, white-tiled preparation table, lay not just one but two chickens. He could hardly believe his luck. There they were: two large chickens done a crispy-brown, oil oozing down on to silver platters, which were heaped with mashed potatoes and mounds of steaming red cabbage. He felt dizzy with desire, the saliva suddenly drooling down his unshaven chin. Indeed he thought he had never felt as much lust for a naked woman's body as he did just now for those chickens.

But Spiv being Spiv was cautious. Down at the far end of the galley there was a skinny cook or assistant in a blue apron tossing ring after ring of German sausage into a vat of boiling water, occasionally reaching in gingerly to pick one up and taste if they were getting done. 'Greedy sod,' Spiv whispered to himself as the German sucked in a half-length of plump pink sausage with a loud noise of appreciation.

He hesitated, trying not to look at those tempting chickens, still sizzling away with a delightful crackling noise of shrinking brown skin. He'd have to nobble the bugger, he told himself. He couldn't nick the birds just like that. He'd be heard and then all hell would be let loose. But how?

Dipping his finger into the steaming hot mound of mashed potatoes and licking it as he crept forward to where the cook kept tossing the rings of sausage into the bubbling vat of hot water, Spiv gripped one of the wooden instruments used to mash boiled potatoes. It would do the job noiselessly, he told himself. Once the cook had gone down for the count he'd be off like greased lightning with those birds. By God, wouldn't he just! Again his mouth started to water at the thought of sinking his teeth into that chicken flesh.

But the ex-barrowboy and graduate of Borstal was not fated to experience that delightful pleasure. Just when he was within striking distance of the unsuspecting cook, there was the great hollow boom of steel striking steel. An acrid smell of scorched metal swept through the galley as the door flew open with the blast, and instruments and pans began to fall from the walls on all sides, and in that same instant Spiv was swept from his feet and went sliding down the abruptly tilting floor.

As the *Vaterland* began to list to port, thick black smoke pouring from the engine room obscuring the bright silver of the spring moon, Bogodan flung up his glasses, ignoring the white tracer being fired wildly from the sinking ship. Already he could see that his plan was working. Dark figures were springing over the sides of the great ship into the boiling sea so far below. Sailors were running and pushing their way through the packed decks heading for the boats. Bogodan nodded his approval. The crew and passengers were doing what he hoped they would. They weren't staying put. Instead, they were abandoning the ship. But not enough of them. He needed more of them in the water, thousands of them if possible. That would keep the planes already being alerted busy and give him his chance of escaping without hindrance.

He cupped his hands around his mouth and shouted to the waiting deck gunners, 'Close up gun crew!'

The men needed no urging. They guessed what the skipper was up to. They wanted to get their murderous task over and done with and be gone. Bogodan waited till they were in position. Raising his Verey pistol, he pressed the trigger. A hush. A rush of air. A crack. Next moment the icywhite flare burst over the stricken ship and the gunners opened fire. The shells of the quick-firer raced towards the *Vaterland* like a glowing white wall. They increased their speed by the instant. They struck home. A radio mast went tumbling down in a blue fury of sparks. Shrapnel hissed everywhere. Glowing an evil, fearsome red, it ripped the deck and superstructure apart. A Fritz machine gun crew disappeared, wiped away as if swatted by a giant hand, to disappear in the white fury of the water below.

The lifeboats started to fall apart. Wires snapped like twine. Boats, splintered into matchwood, lay tangling at crazy angles from the davits. Men and women screamed hysterically, retching and choking as they fell from the boats into the sea below. Some simply collapsed, their lungs ripped apart by that furious volume of fire.

Bogodan stared in horror at his handiwork. The sea around the sinking liner was packed with fighting, shouting, pleading men and women, fighting for their lives, trying to grab something that might support them till rescue came. But there was nothing, and that rescue was not yet underway. He pulled himself together. He had done virtually what he had planned to. It was time to be on his way back to Konigsberg. He bent to the voice tube. 'Fire two!' he cried above the noise of escaping steam and the piteous cries of the dying civilians. The submarine quivered like a live thing. A hiss at the bow and the torpedo was on its way. The sub rose out of the water, relieved of its two-ton burden. Bogodan knew he should order the sub to dive now. But he couldn't. He stood on the bridge as if hypnotized. For he knew it was going to be his dreadful fate to remember this moment, the instant of the 'kill', for the rest of his life. His hands gripped the rim of the conning tower as if rooted there for ever. In his mind he started to count off the seconds till it happened...

Slaughter staggered again. Blood was pouring from the wound at his temple. He didn't even notice it. He had to find and evacuate his people. Time was running out fast. The stricken ship was creaking and groaning like some trapped wild animal in its death throes. From below in the boiler room came a groaning and moaning that boded no good. Everywhere there was panic. Someone was firing a machine gun wildly, not at the submarine but into the crowd of passengers surging to and fro trying to find some kind of escape. Whistles shrilled. Officers bellowed orders that weren't being obeyed.

'Abandon ship!' someone was bellowing through a loud-hailer. *'Abandon ship!'*

Slaughter, shaking his head to clear away the red mist that threatened to overcome him, flashed a look at Rosie and Nellie Dean. The latter had had her pjyama suit blown from her by the blast of the explosion to reveal her emaciated body, all ribs and no breasts. There wasn't a mark on her, but she was dead all right, and she lay clasped in Rosie's arms, as if the latter had been protecting her at the moment of her death. Rosie was dead, too. Slaughter cursed. He had failed the poor devils, he told himself bitterly.

Over at the railing, Corporal Young, holding Lisa, flashed him an enquiring look. Slaughter didn't hesitate. Young could go it alone, he knew. 'Over the side!' he cried above the tremendous racket, the hysterical screams, the wailing of babies, the orders and counter-orders. *'Now!* I'll see to the rest.'

Young didn't hesitate. 'Sir!' he yelled back. Grabbing Lisa by the arm, he tugged hard and they went over the side, plunging into the midst of the others who had already done so, floundering and choking in the icy water of the Baltic.

Slaughter wiped away the blood that was threatening to blind him. He felt giddy. Again he shook his head to clear it and then, crying, 'Spiv – where in hell's name are you, man?' he started to fight his way below.

Again the ship groaned alarmingly. It tilted even further to port. Slaughter, feeling his way below as the lights flickered off and on, knew the *Vaterland*'s days were numbered. She wouldn't last much longer. Already he could hear the water rushing in through the great ragged gash in her hull and the seawater was beginning to lap against his ankles. 'Spiv!' he called again but broke off abruptly.

Spiv was dead. Even in the flickering light he could see that clearly enough. He lay on his back in a circle of his own blood. Next to him lay a platter of food still steaming from the oven. Clasped against his shattered chest he had a roasted chicken, which had a sliver ripped off its breast, with the grease seeping on to his tunic.

'Christ,' he moaned and stopped dead. Of all his men, he had thought that the smart little cockney had been the most likely to survive. Now he, just like the two SOE women who had suffered so much, was dead too. Christ, it wasn't fair. He bent and gently removed the chicken that had cost the ex-barrowboy his life, and in that same instant a voice cried, '*Los, Hande hoch*!'

Slaughter reacted instinctively. Without seeming to aim, he hurled the roast chicken in the direction the voice had come from. Someone yelled. A shot rang out. Slaughter gasped. It was as if someone had thrust a red-hot poker deep into his chest. He staggered back a few paces, trying to keep on his feet. He couldn't. Next moment he crashed into the wall of the galley. Desperately he attempted to keep upright. To no avail. Slowly, the strength ebbing out of his body, as if someone had just opened an invisible tap, he slid down the white tiles, leaving a red trail of blood behind him. In the wavering red haze, Slaughter saw the man in the white cook's uniform towering above him. He seemed very fat and for some reason his hands were very white, as if he had just been working with flour. But they held a rifle. Slowly, very slowly, the man in the white cook's uniform raised it till it was pointing straight at Slaughter's bloody face.

Slaughter heard him speak. He couldn't understand what the man said. It didn't matter. He knew he was going to die and there was nothing he could do about it. He felt very tired, even relaxed, as if he had been expecting this to happen all along – and, in truth, he had. Ever since he had been a wide-eyed but eager second-lieutenant in Palestine back in '36, fighting both Jew and Arab, revelling in what he regarded as a great adventure, he had been anticipating this moment.

Naturally then as a child, he had dreamed that when death in battle came, it would be on a battlefield, where bugles shrilled, banners fluttered and men charged gallantly to their deaths. Death would come through a clean shot through the heart or a bayonet thrust through the chest. It wouldn't happen like this, sprawled on the deck of a sinking ship with the remains of greasy chickens on the floor and a man who looked like a pudgy pastry cook about to blow out his brains. Slaughter's tough, worn face relaxed into a kind of weary smile and he let it happen...

With startling suddenness the *Vaterland*'s main magazine exploded. The great ship was racked from stem to stern. Great gleaming silver fissures began to run the length of her upper deck. Her superstructure creaked and moaned as if under unbearable strain.

Masts and derricks started to tumble down. Smoke belched a deep black from the one stack that was still functioning. Tracer ammunition zig-zagged crazily straight into the sky, turning night into day. She was going down.

A couple of hundred yards away, Corporal Young, holding on tightly to Lisa, kicking off panic-stricken survivors who tried to hang on to them, trod water and stared in shock at the dying ship. Her stern reared higher and higher into the glowing night sky like some sheer metal cliff.

Slowly, inexorably, her bows commenced sliding beneath the sea. Waves leapt up greedily as if to receive this great metal bomb, only to recoil the very next instant, hissing and spluttering angrily. It was as if they could feel the searing heat of her red-hot plates, which were beginning to buckle and explode everywhere under that unbearable pressure.

Next to Young, Lisa freed one hand. It flew to her mouth to suppress her cry. But Young couldn't. He cried, 'Oh my God ... Oh my God!' Then the *Vaterland* gave one last tremendous shudder followed by what seemed like a sigh. Young held his breath. As inexperienced as he was in the ways of the sea, he knew that this was the end.

It was. In one last tumult of wild white water she was gone. One moment the great ship was there; the next she was gone, and the observers quickly became aware that the air was filled with the cries of dying, desperate men. Everywhere there were men – and women – bobbing up and down in the water, waving their hands frantically, trying to keep afloat, attempting to shed their heavy gear before it was too late as the great tidal wave spread from the sunken ship and overwhelmed them.

Young hesitated. What was he to do? Where were the others? But in that confusion, with the living and the dead all around, he knew instinctively that it was hopeless and that Captain Slaughter, wherever he was, would want him to save the girl and himself. 'Come on, Lisa,' he spluttered. 'Let's get out of here ... We'll try and make it to the shore...' He turned and, holding her hand, started to tow her away from the scene of the disaster.

So they departed, swimming by the lone man on a spar, sobbing, sobbing, sobbing, as if his very heart would break. It was over...

Epilogue

It was as the Russian dictator Stalin had commanded: the greatest maritime tragedy of all time. The Russian sinking of the *Vaterland* outdid anything that had gone before it. But this achievement, if it can be called that, did the young patriot Captain Bogodan no good. As soon as Nazi Germany was defeated and Stalin, or 'Uncle Joe' as they were still calling the monster in the West, needed the goodwill of the German people, Bogodan was quietly shipped off to a gulag. He was never heard of again.

In fact, nothing was achieved by the sinking of the *Vaterland* in that last week of World War Two. Friend and foe, they suffered alike to absolutely no purpose. In a moment of despair C, the head of the Secret Intelligence Service, shot his hunters and then, according to some, shot himself. At all events, it's true that after the cremation ceremony, his friends and relatives went off to Ascot and left his still-warm ashes on the top of a cupboard. There they remained for three years until someone recalled what the ugly vase on the cupboard contained.

Naturally, Ian Fleming, the creator of James Bond, prospered. But in the end he didn't particularly like the fame that he had always craved. His world had already disappeared by the time his short life ended in misery. He had his critics, too. One other famous writer of spy novels said of Fleming's books that they were 'cultural pornography', whatever that means.

But we all know what bitchy people writers are, and what normal person takes a blind bit of notice of their pronouncements? For me the important thing was what had happened to those brave young men and women, who had been condemned to death by the secret masters of three nations, German, Russian and British. How had they fared?

Most of them simply vanished when the *Vaterland* had gone to the bottom of the Baltic, taking with her thousands of others of a dozen different nationalities. Even today, sixty years on, their whitened bones are still being washed up on those remote white sandy beaches that fringe the Baltic. Every summer the local newspapers report campers and wandering schoolkids finding new skeletons from the *Vaterland* among the dunes.

Three are known to have survived that terrible tragedy. The tall upper-class radio operator of the SOE, her German-Jewish fellow prisoner, Lisa, and the then SBS greenhorn Corporal Young. The Special Forces Club in London helped me to trace them, but I was informed that they are now very old and perhaps a little ga-ga.

But by the time I had found this out and got to wondering if I should go and see them that famous advance promised by my publisher was beginning to run out. Time, hard booze and the lady in my life had taken their toll. In the end I managed to get one of those 'cheapies', as our railway lines laughingly call them, and I set off to visit – unannounced – Lofty's ancestral home in deepest Somerset. Later I wished I hadn't.

In truth it was a fine early-summer's day when I went there: the kind that makes you think there *is* still something to be said for England as a place to live in. Trees in bud, the birds twittering, wood smoke and the sound of a dog barking in the far distance – that sort of thing, you know.

I was in a bit of a funny mood when I got to the rusty old gates of Lofty's tumbledown pile, with slates from the roof everywhere and the eighteenth-century shutters, sun-bleached and unpainted, hanging at an angle on all sides. I paused there, slightly confused about what I should do next. Should I ring the rusty old metal bell-tug? Should I just walk up the drive, edged on both sides with Victorian ferns?

In the end the decision was made for me. I was alerted by a door creaking rustily and from what I supposed was once the trades-men's entrance one of those old-fashioned basket carriages of the Victorian era made its appearance. In it, sitting bolt upright, as if she was on some sort of a parade, there was an emaciated, very elderly woman, who could be no one else but Lofty.

She nodded to an equally erect old man, who was dressed in khaki of World War Two vintage with two brilliant-white stripes on the upper sleeve of his wartime 'battle blouse'. It could be no other than Corporal Young. He grasped the rusty steering rod of the contraption and pushed, with the aid of a frail old woman, whose hair had once been dyed jet-black, although through neglect it had now become a tobacco-yellow colour. She had to be Lisa.

Slowly, the wobbling front wheel of the carriage creaking alarmingly, they started to come down that neglected overgrown drive towards me, though I doubt if they had seen me yet. Thank God, for of all things, they were actually *singing*. Singing in ancient, cracked voices, their skinny chests heaving alarmingly with the effort as Lofty beat time with her stick.

Instinctively I backed off a few paces. Any sensible man would have. For they were barmy, frighteningly so, there was no denying that. I mean, what were they doing on this fine summer's morning, singing that old Gracie Fields song that the military bands used to play to speed squaddies in their troopships on their way to some foreign battlefield in World War Two. 'Wish Me Luck (As You Wave Me Goodbye)'. They should have been in care. I mean, who was looking after them, the poor sods? Who had allowed them out of that old crumbling house? Why, they ought to have been in some sort of supervised home long ago – surely they deserved that from their country?

They came closer and closer. Now I really got the wind up. I dodged behind the bushes. Still they came on, creaking and warbling down that dark, overgrown drive. Then, just when I thought they'd open the rusty old gate and discover me there, knees trembling, Corporal Young commanded in a reedy voice, 'Parade, parade – *left wheel*!' Lo and behold, all three of them turned smartly and went off in that direction, still singing that old wartime song, only to disappear, vanishing like grey ghosts into the past.

A quarter of an hour later, still shaking, I was in the nearest village pub, spending the last of the advance for my 'epic' on double whiskies to calm my rattled nerves. I didn't even notice some politico on the telly, wearing lipstick and rouge, rabbiting on about how we ought to get slim and eat celery sticks five times a day.

Even now I can't understand what the three of them were about. In the end I just gave up and told myself they were cracked in the head. Perhaps it had something to do with their wartime experiences and the terrible sinking of the *Vaterland*. But there I left it. Outside England didn't look so green and pleasant any more. I pulled up my collar. It was going to rain and I was broke again...